KILLER DEALS AT MAYVIEW MALL

A NOSTALGIACORE COZY MYSTERY

STEVEN TEMPLAR

MYSTERIOUS INK PUBLISHING

Killer Deals at Mayview Mall
A nostalgiacore cozy mystery
By Steven Templar

ART: Cover and chapter header graphics designed by Trevor Sutherland.

To all the 80s and 90s kids

MIXTAPE

Scizzie *- aquatic ambience*
ZAYAZ *- New Approach*
Mitch Murder *- Midnight Mall*
Blank Banshee *- B:/ Start Up*
Jon Secada *- Do You Believe In Us*
New Kids On The Block *- Step by Step*
Toro y Moi *- Girl Like You*
Phoenix *- Trying to Be Cool (A-Trak Remix)*
George Clanton *- I Been Young*
Tiffany *- I Think We're Alone Now*
The Knocks*-Classic (feat. POWERS)*
Runners Club 95 *- Carrie Bradshaw*
Debbie Gibson *- Only in My Dreams*
Sun City,Izzy Perri *- On My Mind*
Jan Hammer *- Crockett's Theme*
Trevor Something *- Do It Again*
Killstarr *- Summer Drive*
Dan Mason *- Go Away*
Thompson Twins *- If You Were Here*

Prologue

THE PUDDLE of oil shimmered atop the asphalt, dazzling neons into prismatic swirls like the Lisa Frank trapper keeper on the passenger seat. The sun was setting yet again, a reminder of another day without answers.

A hushed pair of voices shot across the parking lot, two twenty somethings nervously eyeing me and giggling to themselves close by the abandoned Sizzler steakhouse.

"I swear it's him!" said the man, pocketing his hand after realizing he was pointing aggressively in my direction.

I couldn't hear the partner's response, but from the body language it looked like she didn't agree.

I've been in this position a lot. Enough times to get used to. The question was: did I get recognized for my childhood stint on a cancelled-too-soon nineties sitcom, or for my local Detroit private eye commercials?

"Fine, I'll go ask him," said the woman, now within earshot as she approached.

I feigned a look of surprise, opting to pretend not to be aware of their awkward back and forth. The woman, appearing more of a girl now closer to the driver's side window, crossed her arms and stopped a few feet away. Her steely resolve morphed into apprehension as soon as our eyes met—something I was all too familiar with from my stints on the convention circuit.

"I'm, uhh, my friend over there..." She paused to point back. "He, uhh, are you from that one horror movie with Pacey?"

Color me surprised. After taking a long break from acting, I came out of retirement in the mid-aughts for a few B-movies, which included a horror flick that gained a decent cult following. These days though, not many people remember it aside from the diehards and con-goers.

After confirming my identity to the antsy woman, she called her friend over for a quick selfie.

"Hey, thanks, my roommate's never gonna believe this!" the younger man said. "Hey, is it true you're investigating that murder at Mayview Mall?"

News spreads fast. The Channel 7 van was hot on the scene before the body wasn't. I hoped my name wouldn't be attached, at least not yet. I'd rather be billed as the one that solved the mystery.

"Shame what happened," I said, not answering the question. "I hope they figure out whodunnit. It was nice seeing you!"

I locked the car and shot them a smile before strolling away. Working the case? You bet I was. Someone would have to pay for what they did to the girl of my dreams. Little did I know, things were about to get a whole lot weirder.

Chapter 1

A FEW DAYS EARLIER...

I hiked up the aging sloped parking lot as a tangerine orb fell behind the sprawling complex. Purposely parking the DeLorean further away gave more time to soak in the panoramic view of the once bustling shopping center. Mayview Mall opened in the Summer of '76 to the fanfare of Metro Detroit's clamoring public. Offering dozens of stores through its two levels of shopping bliss, what stood before me was a far cry from the black-and-white photo hung on my apartment wall.

"Mall's closed, buddy," a high-pitched, possibly teenage voice said.

The silhouette had little defining features, blurred by the thick frosted glass entry doors. I took a step back and shook my head. The Casio on my wrist showed it was just past eight, although the mid-summer skyline made it feel much earlier. Etching next to the doors confirmed the mall closed at eight on weekdays—hours literally set in the gray and brown stone that covered most of the building.

The lanky shape shrank away before I had the chance to reply. Nothing that a few more fierce raps of my knuckles couldn't solve.

The voice grew louder and more agitated. "I said we're closed!"

"I'm here for an interview," I lied. Well, is it a lie if the owner encouraged the cover story?

A pause followed by an "Oh" and one of the doors cracked to

reveal a pale white, acne covered face, solidifying my self proclaimed title of Detroit's Greatest Gumshoe.

The teen's eyes darted to the empty lot behind and settled on the Boblo Island logo across my chest. Either he was a fan of old amusement parks or eye contact wasn't his thing. Or he was just on edge, realizing I could be his future boss.

"You shoulda said so," he said while overcorrecting his posture. "Ms. Cunningham is waiting for you, sir."

Sir. I don't turn forty-one for another few months—I wasn't ready to be seen as someone's senior. At least my body still felt every bit of thirty, minus the general aches and pains I've collected. Comes with the territory. And keeping up on the weekly P90X workout takes a toll.

"Come on in." The youngster waved me through and locked the door behind. "You're a bit early. I wasn't expecting you just yet."

If being fifteen minutes late meant early, then I wouldn't have spent countless days in the principal's office. Two decades later, memories of that old musty room still gave me chills. My guide looked distracted, leading me to believe he wasn't even aware of the time.

Normally, I'd meet a client in my office. But this wasn't a normal case and the dust was still settling in my new HQ. I hadn't even stopped by to take the shrinkwrap off the new pinball machine I bought for the waiting room. Otherwise, the office was mostly finished, aside from a few final touches left on the surprisingly artsy TGIF TV show mural. So, I had exaggerated the construction, *just a tad*—but it gave me an excuse to peek behind the scenes at one of my favorite childhood hangouts. And I justified the lie by telling myself it would be good to get an early preview of what I was getting myself into.

I followed the teen, whose name I learned was Bart, through the bleak white hallway—out of place compared to the dated late seventies aesthetic outside. Glossy framed photos advertised an assortment of shops—a tinge of sadness passed over after recognizing most of the stores had closed or moved to strip malls throughout the city or across the road. The mall was like many across the country: struggling to survive against the rise of online shopping and the gradual change of shopping habits.

"So, what's your name, sir?" Bart asked as we left the hallway, opening to the main area of the mall.

The wide open expanse took me by surprise—I had been here hundreds of times, but this was my first private, after hours tour. And it had been at least a year since my last visit. I shook my head —I was part of the problem. It was just too easy to shop online.

Lost in the dim lights of nostalgia, I almost missed Bart repeating the question. "Oh sorry. The name's Paul. Paul Washington."

"Well Paul, just head up to the second floor. Main office is past the bathrooms in the food court." He pointed to my destination, one I was already familiar with. "Think you can get there yourself? I need to make sure the stragglers have filed out."

I nodded and thanked the young security guard, then strolled over to the escalators—off like most of the electricity in the building. The fading sun provided enough light, pouring through the ample skylights beaming from the ceiling high above. Bart was one lucky kid. I remembered dreaming of working at the mall in my early years. In high school, a job at the mall was about as cool as it got. To this day, my good friend Corey still recounts how awesome it was, parading his employee discount at the Harmony House like one of life's crowning achievements. Catch him on the right day and he'd tell you how all the kids would hook each other up with savings. And hook up with each other, too. Yeah, Bart was a lucky dude, although he probably didn't realize how cool he was to the old white guy wandering the cream tiled floors.

I climbed the stairs next to the frozen escalators, feeling the worn carpet under my sneakers. Carpet was a bad design call for a place frequented by teens, at least at one point. The blue circles and red triangles on the jazzy black flooring on the other hand—that *was* a good design choice. On the way up, faint rumblings of an old Michael McDonald song fought to escape from the aging overhead speaker system. Despite the muffled, warbling vaporwave-like sound, the music matched the empty stretches of lonely stores.

The second floor looked much like the first, aside from the glass railing overlooking the shops below. Or at least what was left of them. Since I was apparently early, according to Bart, a few extra minutes wandering the halls couldn't hurt. On the way to the food court, I counted seven active stores in the wing, and about double that closed. Most were sad empty shells of history, with a few used to display other businesses hanging on to their existence. The three other wings likely looked the same, or maybe even worse.

The food court didn't help assuage any guilt. Only three fast-food restaurants remained, including a *Sqarro* Pizza, one of the letters clearly flipped. The owner must have grown tired of franchise licensing fees, I guess. Marinara lingered in the air as I walked through the ambitious, if not excessive seating. The whole area didn't even exist at one point. Decades ago, instead of fast-food joints and a broken carousel, the county's coolest arcade took its place. The two-story *Tilt* was the place to be for a kid in the eighties and nineties. With only neons glowing throughout the dark, crowded game rooms, it looked more like the hangout for the Foot Clan in the original *Turtles* movie. But instead of young misguided thieves, a majority of the patrons' worst offense was skipping school to play the newest 2D fighting game, or maybe snatching a few quarters from mom to play pinball. Just like the malls of America, arcades weren't doing so hot.

Off in the distance, an older man pushed an equally ancient looking floor scrubber. We locked eyes, and the long gray-haired janitor nodded softly, continuing on his polishing path. Materializing from thin air, a dark suited man stalked towards the cleaner with purpose, throwing up his hands and barking orders. The janitor stopped the machine and pulled off his yellow corded headphones and stared back. With folded arms and squinted eyes, he was clearly not buying whatever the pony-tailed business man was selling. The exchange was brief, likely due to the elder man smiling back politely, agreeing to whatever was hurled at him. With only this context, the suit came off as a villain. Especially since he looked like the one from the third Karate Kid movie. I sauntered on, hoping I wouldn't find myself in his warpath. For his sake, not mine.

Pressing on, a row of coin-operated faux leather massage chairs caught my attention. The small orange out of order signs reminded me nothing was safe these days. Why did I take this case again? Another reminder of when I got the call last week—excitement mixed with a giant heap of nostalgia and dollop of sadness. It's not every day a mall owner calls for help to find whoever's playing a fast one with the books. Game on.

Chapter 2

THE CRAMPED OFFICE had a faint smell of cigarettes, masked by the flowery scent coming from the woman in the red dress. The mix of bergamot and rose was unmistakable: White Diamonds—the perfume my ex-wife adored well into the last few years of our marriage.

A few years older than my former flame, the woman was stunning from head to toe. A bit too done up for my tastes, but it didn't take a detective to realize she probably made most men swoon, as well as the ladies. Flowing auburn hair matched the sundress, tightly cinched at her waist to show off her curves. *Did she always wear this much makeup to work, I wondered.*

She peeled off a pair of thin cherry-red rimmed glasses, chewing gently on one of the arms while her unnaturally blue eyes took a long walk up and down my body. Damn. I'd been a private eye for a few years now, and this was my first time encountering The Woman In The Red Dress trope I'd secretly wished for. No, she wasn't my type. But she was gorgeous, and I'd need to pull out a calendar to figure out the last time I'd been on a proper date. *Focus, Paul.* Gorgeous never worked out for the private eyes, as I'm sure Sam Spade would warn.

Three little words came laced with authority. Not just words, a command. "Have a seat." She motioned to the single folding chair across from her worn office desk. Her voice could only be described as sultry. And provocative. This woman knew how to get what she wanted. Tiffany Cunningham. No stranger to the local fifty under fifty list, the businesswoman was known as an entrepreneur, philanthropist, and part-time model. I did my research. A coy smile eased across her evenly golden face. *Tanning booth or vacationer?* Detroit got some sun, but it was too early in the season for the white woman to be that bronze.

My back settled against the hard plastic. "Nice place you got here, ma'am."

She leaned into the plush leather executive chair to cross her long legs, bumping the back into the yellow-ish beige wall behind. "For now at least. That's why I need your help."

The chair looked expensive and out of place, just like her. This room was small, stinky, and relatively barren. In addition to the furniture, the only items of note were her MacBook, a heavy safe, and an aging filing cabinet that looked like it came with the place. Oh, and a shelf of dense gold trophies—Businesswoman of the Year, no doubt.

I tried to hide my curiosity—everything felt... *off.* "Your assistant said there's been some," I paused, for no reason in particular, other than trying to place the echoes of a Tears for Fears song playing overhead outside her office, "financial issues."

The smile disappeared, traded for an exquisite display of eyelash flutters so fierce I swore a small breeze carried over. Her voice changed, a younger, sweeter southern drawl. "Good help is hard ta' find these days." The smile returned, proudly.

I didn't hide my disdain for being deceived. "Nice accent. You could be on TV with that accent."

Things were off indeed. Why'd she lie to get me here? The thought of getting up and leaving crossed my mind. Until remembering she was offering three times my going rate, with per diem. And I could use a break from tailing cheating spouses and catching insurance fraudsters gaming the system. This was my first real case.

What you'd call a bonafide mystery—and what I got into the private eye business for. Adding in the opportunity to get a backstage pass at my old stomping grounds kept my butt glued.

Her voice returned to the normal raspy seductress. "I'm sorry I tricked you." Her words lacked any signs of authenticity. The baby blues drifted down to the desk. "When I called, I got nervous and well, here we are. The offer still stands."

Nervous, her? File that away for later. "So you said someone's been stealing from you?"

"Straight to the point. Good, I like that." A manicured glittery nail twirled through the mass of auburn strands. With each pass, the bundle became tighter and tighter until she paused, looking up with a flirtatious gaze more suited for the club than business. "Over the past few months, the numbers haven't been adding up."

"Business doesn't seem so hot."

"Thanks, *detective.*" If she was upset, it didn't show. "You know why I called you?"

I scratched my stubbly chin. Damn, forgot to shave again. "Testing my memory from the call? Someone's fudging the numbers. Taking more than their share. Office Space kind of stealing, from the sound of it."

An authentic sounding laugh. I figured she'd get the percentage-stealing movie callback. "Well yes. But more specifically, you."

Damn. Here we go. I wasn't ashamed of being a former actor—hell, before the pandemic I would hit up the conventions now and then to catch up with old showbiz friends. The rising costs of renting a booth and a continued fade into obscurity made it easier to stay home. So as that chapter wrapped up, focusing on the detective gig had my attention. I often missed connecting with the real fans, though.

I played stupid, something that came easy. "Saw my ad on TikTok?"

That earned an eye roll. "There's quite a few private *dicks* in the area. You're the only one that seems obsessed with malls and old technology. I figured it might give you a better perspective of what I'm facing here."

Welp, there goes my ego assuming things. "You've read my articles for the Sentry?" The local newspaper got an article or five from me each year—whenever they needed an opinion on something to draw in the Xennial crowd. Verbatim what the editor told me. *I couldn't use that word without thinking of burning a CD.*

Her lips curved up. "And you were just so cute in that movie with what's his name, the prom king guy... oh, Freddie!"

And there it was. First instincts rarely lead me astray. And right now, the woman in the red dress was buttering me up a bit too thick for how much she's paying—especially for a business losing money. A fan? Sure. But this case appears cut and dry and the diamond rock on her finger was blinding. Outside perceptions are one thing, but from everything I've read, Tiffany and her husband were couple of the year.

"Nice ring."

No signs of embarrassment, interesting.

"Thanks." She held out her hand, staring at the shiny rock like it was the first time. "I appreciate your directness, Mr. Washington." The flirtatiousness dialed down just a few ticks on the stereo.

I sucked air through my teeth. "So, what do you need from me?"

"Business isn't as bad as it looks. Well, okay, it's bad. But I have some plans to revitalize the mall and we're still in the black. For now."

A ding chimed from her wrist, pulling her attention to the smart watch like Dick Tracy. Her face scrunched up. *Anger?* Eyes shot back across the desk.

"Sorry, always something. Where were we? Oh yes. Year over year, we aren't declining too drastically. But whatever is going on is only making things worse. It started at least three months ago.

When I first noticed, it was just a few thousand dollars. We still take cash from some of our tenants. This safe under here..." She stopped and shot a come-hither look, pointing under the desk, hopefully at the safe. "We keep the money in here until a biweekly pickup from an armored car company. The first time it happened, we assumed they messed up."

"Makes sense. So you called the cops?"

The redhead shook her head. "Bad publicity is not always good publicity. We fought with them for a bit until we decided to settle and end our contract."

"Good job keeping it under wraps. I didn't hear a peep."

"Exactly. But it happened again. This time, even more money. Almost a week's profit."

I traced a finger down my nose. "So business isn't that bad, huh? That's a lot of money to put in a safe. A safe that was already tampered with."

She folded her arms over her chest. "I don't like your tone, detective. You're working for me, remember?"

"So I'm officially hired? Then you're paying me to figure this out. I'm going to look at all the angles."

She leaned forward, rolling out the tension in her body. "You're right. But I thought ahead. Camera." She pointed to a small black orb in the ceiling. "And I changed the combination."

"With the outside company out, that limits your suspects." I pointed to the tiny back sphere above her head. "What's your eye in the sky tell you?"

"A *power glitch.*" She emphasized the words with air quotes. "Lost a few hours of footage in this room and around the food court."

"Hell of a coincidence."

"Hell of a coincidence," she repeated, nodding her head. "I'd rather handle this all in house and not get the police involved. I'll give you a week to see what you can find. And then I'm turning it over to them."

"Sounds fair. I'm going to need carte blanche here," I said dryly, burying the eagerness of having free rein over the mall. "Access to the mall, the staff, the cameras, the little hallways behind the shops. Even the old secret tunnels underneath."

She slowly ran teeth over her bottom lip. "Already started the investigation, huh? Consider it done."

Chapter 3

"IT WAS like she had some kind of hold on me," I said, nestling my shoulders into the fluffy microfiber couch.

"You mean like a vampire," Geri said matter-of-factly. She broke eye contact to spritz the nearest plant with a spray bottle. "The next question is, what sort of vampire are we talking about?"

I couldn't hold back a chuckle. "I'm serious, Ger."

"I'm serious too. It changes your approach. We talking Kiefer in *Lost Boys*? Or maybe Anne Rice vampires?" She continued misting the plants, petting them lightly to watch the leaves bounce.

Gardenia "Geri" Wilcox was my neighbor. Apartment 227 across the hall in a modern, cozy building a few minutes from downtown Detroit. For the last few months, I found myself decompressing in her quirky little studio apartment more than my own. It was perfect—close, good company, and the setting had all the right vibes, as the kids would say. The budding botanist, *pun intended,* had flowers and plants from wall to serene blue wall. The giant fish tank alone was enough to put my mind at ease, watching the beautiful azure betta fish dancing through the underwater castles. Between the greenery, bright pink and blue neons adorned the walls with catchy phrases like "Relax" and "Outatime". It was everything I wished my place was: Judge Reinhold's digs from the second *Beverly Hills Cop* movie, minus all the guns. Since Geri's girlfriend was always on extended work trips, the arrangement was mutual—I kept her from getting lost in her thoughts, and the super chill apartment helped me forget the rat race of chasing down cheaters.

I set the smooth, iced green tea on a star shaped coaster. Geri always had a pitcher of delicious, healthy potions. "She's just all kinds of wrong and something's not right here. I can't put my finger on it."

She set down the bottle and crossed her brown tattoo-covered arms, her dark eyes narrowing. "From what I'm hearing, it sounds like you'd like to." Her pierced eyebrow shot up to match the crooked smile.

"Hey, despite what you think, I'm not trying to get with anyone right now. You were the first woman I had a decent conversation with in months and…"

"Yeah, yeah. The divorce." She smiled and grabbed the spray bottle, resuming a mini rainfall in the jungle-themed room.

Geri loves to tease me about it whenever she can. She swears I was making a pass at her, but I have a much different story. Despite the hiccup, the bohemian horticulturist had become as reliable a friend as they get. A bit aloof and spacey, but smarter than most of the people in my life. And there aren't many. Other than Corey, she completes the tiny inner circle of friends.

"Okay pretties, I'll be back later," she said, petting the top of a fern as if it was a second grader going off to school. After a few taps on her phone, a soft melodic outrun track buzzed from the bookcase speakers scattered around the apartment. "They love Mark Dee. It's their favorite right now."

I rolled my eyes and finished the tea. Man, whatever she put in this was ethereal.

"Back to business." The raven haired woman jumped over the loveseat, plopping down to face me, criss-cross applesauce. "So if she's not a vampire, what's got you in a tizzy?"

"I mean, good question. The mall for one. She's the owner of the most magical place from my childhood. Can nostalgia do that?"

That pesky eyebrow shot up again. "You're the detective, detective. Here's what I think. You said she was very clearly flirting with you. You're not used to people being direct with you. In fact, most people you meet in your kind of work are downright liars and thieves. The nostalgia thing is definitely clouding things, and she hit your ego up by doing some digging on you. So in a nutshell, she made you feel wanted, known, and threw in some emotional manipulation."

"Putting that psych degree to good use. Now I remember why I come here."

She winked. "Hey every now and then, the past comes crawling back." She raised her hands to the ceiling, as if presenting the room. "Now it's all about the plants, babe."

I tend to forget that Geri was a psychotherapist before becoming a full-time traveling plant doctor. That free-spirit and extra youthful appearance made it easy to believe she didn't have a care in the world, unless it was something green.

I propped an elbow on the cushion to hold up my thought-filled head. "Why go through all of that, though? She's paying good money from the get."

"Again, you're the detective here. Do I have to do all the work for you?" She shook her head, sending the dark wavy hair bouncing. "It's a power thing. You don't get to be Tiffany freaking Cunningham by sitting on the sidelines. She's ensuring your loyalty."

"In addition to giving me a job and a fat paycheck? Interesting. You sure you don't want to tag along for this one?" I was only half joking—Geri had a knack for reading people and would be a real asset. And I didn't want to blow my first serious job. The dream of being a police consultant on the big cases was at risk, after all—if that was even a real possibility.

"Sorry sweetie. She sounds like a riot, but I've got a dispensary in the U.P. that's paging Dr. Greenthumb." She poked her thumbs up, wiggling them at my face. "Heading up tomorrow, I'll let you know if I get back early."

I've never known anyone that could go from astute psychoanalyst to slapstick goofball in seconds, and the neighbor sure grew on me. I took a refill of the delicious liquid and strolled across the hall to my apartment. More anticipation than nervousness followed me into the bedroom. I needed to ensure a good night's rest—and movies always knocked me out like a baby. I plucked a worn copy of the 1980s classic *Chopping Mall,* popping it into the equally worn VHS player. Hopefully, the next few days were free of malfunctioning killer security robots. Before the beginning credits finished, I drifted into a deep sleep, thinking about my first shift as Head of Security of Mayview Mall.

Chapter 4

FORGOING the 'good to the last drop' instant coffee on my shelf, I sprung for the expensive stuff from the tiny mall Starbucks. If the mall was dying, this coffee shop had something to say about it. Nestled between one of the four sneaker stores and a Penny's, the café was bumping—and the mall hadn't technically even opened for the day. From the look of it, every patron was on staff in the giant shopping center. One perk of working at Mayview, I guess.

"Iced coffee for... *Kuffs*?" The barista's tone showed no sign they caught the reference to Christian Slater's early 90s *Beverly Hills Cop* wannabe flick. To be fair, it was a deeper cut than most of my aliases.

I sipped the coffee, savoring the bitter, black iced goodness. "Okay, Bart. Where were we?"

"First, I'll take you to the security room. That's probably where you'll be most of the time anyway."

Tiffany had assigned the young security guard to give a detailed tour, complete with an introduction to anyone important. Little did he know, the post-it stuck to the inside of my scratchy polyester slacks had the names of all her suspects—anyone who could have access to the safe or her office. *Man these pants were uncomfortable.* After today, I'd be ditching this uniform.

I fought the urge to tug at the heavy fabric and shifted in the seat. "What makes you say that? There's a lot of ground to cover in a place this big."

A voice called for Bart from the register.

The guard sprang up to grab a giant green cup off the counter, fist bumping a barista on the return trip. I hadn't even noticed him order. Free coffee? Corey would love to hear that the mall's hookup culture was alive and strong.

My junior assistant took a swig and nodded with a smile before finally answering the question. "Last guy in charge of security barely moved from that room."

It still hadn't sunk in that I was in charge. All part of the ruse—the owner thought it made more sense than telling everyone a private eye was snooping around. She was right, of course. Drawback was, I might end up loving the gig too much.

"Well, you don't have to worry about that with me." I followed the slender guard past a non-functioning water fountain set smack dab in the middle of the mall. "I plan to be as hands on as it gets."

Bart stopped to look back with a puzzled expression before continuing forward. "You know, I looked you up online. I found your website. You were some kind of detective. Why take this job?"

As I was about to open my mouth, the mall PA system clicked on, startling me more than I'd like to admit. "Gooood mornin' Mayview!"

My guide paused once more, raising his index finger to the ceiling.

Across the open floor, a light smattering of claps and a few whistles escaped from the remaining stores. I caught the annoyed expression on a heavyset man as he unlocked the sliding doors to a shoe store.

"I can't hear you! I said gooood morrrrnnnin' Mayview!" The woman's voice belted from above.

Even less applause followed an audible groan. An elderly man in dire need of a morning coffee threw his head back and belted, "Shut up! Shut up!" to the heavens before he returned to haphazardly adjusting phone cases at a kiosk.

"What the..." I looked around, trying to make sense of what I just heard, other than an obvious throwback to a classic eighties war comedy.

"Miss Debbie is kind of a dork. You have a lot in common. I think you'll get along with her. C'mon, let me show you the employee entrance."

Only in young Bart's presence for less than an hour, and he's throwing shade. From his body language and tone, I doubt he realized it. But he wasn't wrong—nerd, dork, geek, all terms of endearment for yours truly.

The employee area was just as I imagined: sterile grey corridors running parallel to the mall. Thick, poorly labeled metal doors led to each store. Compared to the rest of the mall's dated condition, the hallways were spotless, recently painted, and well-lit. Every few feet had one of those cheesy motivational posters my middle school librarian loved. I thought back to Corey's stories, imagining the hijinks that must have taken place here, away from the prying eyes of the public.

"Do employees use this?" I said, pointing to the large open room. It was sparse: a few dated brown vending machines, steel lockers, and three of the plastic folding tables you'd find at a kid's birthday party.

"Sometimes. We kept having people stealing from the lockers, so we installed some cameras back here. Since then, people seem to eat in their cars or in the back of their stores." Bart took a double take at a vending machine and let out an audible yelp. "Zagnut! My favorite!"

He ran over to the machine, fumbling for quarters, completely missing my Beetlejuice impersonation.

"They must have just stocked these!" Bart mumbled, lips smacking loudly while he inhaled the peanut butter and toasted coconutty bar. Kid had good taste.

"I didn't even know they made those anymore."

The youngster's eyes lit up. "Oh let me tell you!"

And he did. My comment opened a door that didn't close all

day. As Bart continued the tour, I learned about his favorite chocolate confections, received a history of the candy trade in the States, and got the hottest tips on where to score Canadian chocolate here in Detroit. It was interesting, but through the meandering tour, I would learn one thing was sure: I'd bet my Las Vegas Pinball Hall of Fame hat that the kid wasn't the thief.

Near the end of the winding hall sat the security office. Inside, the small room was dark and freezing. A cool air-conditioning breeze tickled my nose, wafting a scent that always carried me to the early days of summer and my family's tradition: battling the heat as long as possible before switching on the AC. One year we almost made it to July 4th—something I wouldn't recommend during a sweaty Midwest heatwave.

The light tones of John Secada brought me back from memory lane. "Just Another Day" gently thumped from an old Magnavox CD player on the desk near the monitors. While Bart scurried around to clean a mess of fast food containers, my eyes drifted to the glow of the screens.

Ten dated monitors huddled closely together in what was once the top of the line in CCTV security. In the eighties. At the edge of the setup, four outer screens remained static, focused on the exterior doors to the mall. Occasionally, one would flip to the parking lot, in all its grayscale pixelated glory. The rest of the screens displayed views from inside. These color screens cycled through various angles, capturing the day's first loop of mall walkers passing employees readying for the slow influx of Friday morning patrons.

I studied the cameras, thinking about Tiffany's report of a mysterious power outage taking out the system. "Hey Bart, you guys ever have any issues with these cameras?"

"What do you mean?"

"You know the usual. Missed recordings, power outages, that sort of thing."

"Recordings? I only found out last week that the dang things haven't been recording for months now. Finally got them to work, but I have to set it each morning. The power outages are kinda normal around here, though. I have to go and reboot the system. Here, I'll show ya."

Bart walked me through how simple it was to reset the computer controlling the cameras—and chatted during the long wait for it to boot back, complete with *Windows 95* startup jingle. I clocked just over six minutes until the CRT screens flickered back to life. If someone knew their way around here, they could have easily bought themselves enough time to rush over to Tiffany's office for a crack at the safe without being seen. I made a mental note to time the trek—and find out more about the curious recording situation.

The young guard resumed his mission of making the dim room spotless, now wiping smudges off the tinted one-way window looking out into the bland employee corridor. I resumed studying the live footage, learning I could tap on the crusty Gateway 2000 branded keyboard to pause on certain feeds and even zoom in.

The track on the CD player changed to another Secada hit, "Do You Believe in Us" played twice as loud.

And then I saw her.

Wavy brown hair bounced off her shoulders while she danced the silliest looking cabbage patch. I tried zooming in, only coming close enough to catch a slight glimpse at the dark-rimmed glasses on her smiling, warm amber face. I'd seen hundreds of beautiful women over the years, and a few this week, but right now I wasn't seeing—I was feeling. Time slowed to a crawl while I forgot how to breathe, lost in my very only *Can't Hardly Wait* dreamgirl reveal.

I tapped on the screen. "Wh-Who's that?"

"Huh?" Bart yelled across the room over the music and glassy whistles from scrubbing furiously at the window.

After a third attempt, I realized it was fruitless and mashed at the CD player until the music paused. "Her." I pointed again at the screen, leaving a fingerprint. "Who is... *she*?" My words trailed off as I became a believer in love at first sight.

Bart's already pale face drained of color as he scrambled to the Magnavox. I looked over to see the woman had stopped dancing, wearing a look of confusion while pointing at the ceiling.

"That's the PA system. You just said that to the whole mall." He hit a few buttons and returned to face me, crossing his arms. "Boss, leave the music to me. And that's Miss Debbie, the next person you're going to meet."

Chapter 5

BART SURE WAS a stickler for rules. If I really were his boss, I would be proud to have such a dedicated employee. But in this case, it worked against me—I really wanted to use the employee entrance to the bookstore, but the teen said it was for emergency use only, even for the security team. Apparently, one too many overzealous guards had scared workers in the past by barging through the back doors.

The jaunt through the mall was pleasant, added by the morning sunlight pouring in from the overhead skylights. A sweet smell of cinnamon rolls wafted from deep within the giant building making my mouth water. I wondered if the employees ever got used to that smell.

"Sleuths is just over here," Bart said, picking up speed as he rushed past a small atrium of beautiful pink and green flowers.

Sleuths was the aptly named mystery-themed bookstore. And what a cool sight it was, standing out from the rest of the typical stores. From the outside, dark mahogany wood paneling encased old fifties style bay windows. A quick peek inside showed the same style flooring throughout the store. Only open for an hour, a middle eastern man in his early twenties lay curled up inside under the window, hardcover book in one hand, steaming hot mug in the other. The build-out must have cost a fortune—I'd know, just having dropped a pretty penny on my new office in downtown Detroit.

"Miss Debbie should be here. It's like her second home," Bart said, motioning to follow inside.

As soon as I set foot on the first wood plank, a smile crept over my face. Smooth chill beats of a synth track massaged my ear drums. The sweet warbly instrumental track transported me back to the early nineties, the era I was most fond of—eighties taking a close second.

Walls of alternating black and dark crimson brick further set the mood, lightly reflecting the glow of purple LED rope lights wrapped around the ceiling. No wait—pink lights. Neat, they slowly cycled through gentle colors, melting relaxing hues over the four long aisles of heavy oak bookcases. Deeper into the store, I clocked about half the shelves were filled with mystery novels, some appearing quite old judging by the layer of dust caked on the worn binding. I caught a few notable new releases, from romance to fantasy. They even had my favorite time travel series from an indie author that grew up in the area.

"Wow," I said quietly to myself. "What a cool place."

"Thanks," a soft feminine voice startled me from behind.

I guess I said it louder than I thought.

"Hey Miss Debbie." Bart approached, joining the short woman hovering by my shoulder.

The girl from the camera. No nineties adult contemporary this time. Instead, the music overhead faded into another vaporware track, this one slower, more melodic, with a rumbling rhythm—almost sensual. My heart skipped a beat—she was even prettier up close.

"Hey Bart. I keep telling you, just Deb! I'm too young for Miss. This the new guy?" A single eyebrow popped over her black-rimmed glasses, the hazel eyes scanning me as if to say "Is that it?" The thought lines soon faded away on her light brown skin, replaced by the warm smile accompanying the hand held out in greeting.

I took her hand with a firm shake. "Hey there, Deb, is it?"

Her handshake was just as tight, but soft and gentle at the same time.

"So, you're our new head of security." Was that a hint of disdain in her voice? "Glad you like the place. I've always wanted to own a bookstore. A place that's not just for reading, but for hanging out." She motioned to the man chilling at the window, who took notice and raised his coffee in return. "That's Hakim. He works the weekends, but I guess the vibes are just too hard to resist."

"Cool... *vibes*, I dig it." I've been known to use the common lingo, for an older guy. I wondered, just how old was she? She looked a little younger, but I figured… I *hoped* she was around my age. This woman had my detective skills in a frenzy. *What was with this case?*

She wiggled her nose like Samantha on Bewitched and the cute smile faded. "That *is* what the kids say, isn't it?" The smile came back, just as the lights morphed into a soft electric yellow and began a slow blink, leaving us in brief moments of darkness.

She turned back to the off duty employee and yelled out. "Hakim!"

The man shrugged, then jumped to attention, springing into action on his day off. The store was now completely dark, aside from the interior mall light leaking from the entrance.

"What's going on?" I said, squinting to make any detail in almost pitch darkness.

"Sorry," she said. "We have this murder mystery event on the weekends. It's supposed to be random, but we usually have it an hour or two before closing on Friday and Saturday nights. The lights will slowly dim and flicker a bit, and one of us is found *'dead'*." She added air quotes. "The customers love it. They try to figure out Whodunnit, and all that. I've had a few actors from the local improv troupe stop in to play the suspects." A look of playful annoyance crossed her face. "But *someone* has been messing with the settings. Right, Hakim?"

"I'm sorry boss!" Hakim said on his way to the back. "It should have been disabled until the weekend!"

"Yeah, yeah," Deb said. "Hakim proposed to his fiancé last weekend in the store. It was actually super cute. The lights turned off, and when they came back on he was on one knee, big glowing ring and all."

Bart looked at his watch, tapping his foot impatiently. I got the sense he was ready to rush us to the next person on my list.

"Right out of a romance novel," I said dryly.

"Not a fan?" She cocked her head, sending some dark brown strands of wavy hair bouncing.

"I'm more of a mystery fan myself. I see you have some originals."

"Ahem," Bart interjected with a loud cough. "We really need to be moving along now."

"You should stop by sometime," she said, with just a touch of a hair twirl. "You're welcome to take a look."

I'd be back, that was for sure. She was a tough cookie to read, but there was something going on there. At least on my end.

"Why'd you rush us outta there?" I said, following Bart to the next shop on the list.

"I have rounds to make, boss. Tiffany said to introduce you, and that's what we're doing. You can flirt on your own time."

"Woah, Bart!" I made a hard stop next to the fountain, almost bumping into an older couple making a wish. I watched their penny plop into the pool before continuing. "Wait. Do you think she was flirting with me?" I instantly questioned taking social advice from the teen—he was no Dr. Drew, and this certainly wasn't an episode of Loveline.

"C'mon, boss. I don't know what else to call all that book talk.

Plus I remember her talking about you before you were hired. You can head back after we're done if you want. But right now we need to get moving. I have places to be now that I'm the only guard for this whole place."

So maybe there really was something there with Debbie? I smiled to myself, wondering what kinds of things Bart overheard.

"Boss!" My guide shouted, abruptly breaking the dream sequence.

The kid was dedicated. And apparently stretched thin after the outside company was fired. I'd have to make sure to give him some kind of made up award before I left my post as the fake security director.

While fun, the rest of the tour was uneventful. I met with a few store managers—everyone that would have been in the mall during or before the most recent theft. None had as much personality as Debbie, aside from Gary Tripper, the record store owner. Gary seemed way too happy to meet me and gave the impression he was just that excited all the time. I left with a free vinyl from one of my favorites—a 'til Tuesday record. Gary said my money was no good there, immediately offering a 'friends and family' discount, despite only knowing me for a few minutes.

After meeting all the key suspects, Bart told me his job was done and drifted off for lunch before the all-important rounds. Good kid, unless that was an act. *Was it?* My gut said he really was that genuine.

So far, I didn't have much to go on. Time was ticking, with only a few days left before Tiffany would be calling in the cops. Record store Gary and Bart seemed innocuous, if not transparent to a fault. Sofie, the manager at the jewelry store, was all business and too wrapped up in her Chanel purse to be bothered. And Maxwell, the owner of the cell phone repair kiosk, didn't strike me as a thief—and only because it was relevant, the slow saunter and reliance on his cane dropped him low on the suspect list. Whoever was behind this would need access to the security office to reset the cameras, and be spry enough to make a mad dash to the manager's room to make the swipe. That ruled out the cellphone guru.

The day had sadly proved Debbie and her hazel eyes were high on the suspect list. Bart had mentioned she made the mall greetings every morning on the PA—*inside the security office*. She didn't strike me as the thieving type, but which good crook did, anyway? After timing the brisk walk from the security room to the safe, a quick three minutes—I decided to pay the bookstore owner another visit.

Chapter 6

IT WAS JUST past seven after all my "work" duties were completed—the fake ones, not the real sleuthing. Which, as fate had it, was the theme of the bookstore I was looking at. Before my shelltop crossed into the glowing ambiance of the wood pulp palace, the mall queen slid between, blocking a second meeting with the girl of my eighties movie dreams. And, unfortunately, suspect number one.

"I'm glad I caught you," Tiffany said, lowering her voice to a whisper. "How's the investigation going?"

"Just getting the lay of the land. You have an interesting group of characters here." I tried to hide my frustration while peeking over her shoulder to see if Debbie was in the store. No dice.

"Robbie unlovingly refers to them as the Gang of Misfit Toys. From some old Christmas movie."

"It's Island of," I corrected her. "Who's Robbie?"

"Huh?" she asked, clearly not a fan of Rankin and Bass. "Robert. My uncle. I left him off your list on purpose. Especially because Bart's on thin ice with him. Who knew an argument about Snickers bar ingredients could cause someone to lose it? That's my uncle."

"I've known him less than a week, and I can safely say that sounds like the Bart I know. So uncle Rob has a bit of a temper?" I thought back to yesterday, the ponytail in a suit scolding the janitor.

"That's putting it lightly. It's time you hear the whole story. I get not wanting the details, none of my bias influencing you. But now that you've met most of the suspects," she paused and looked around, realizing her voice had risen from the whisper. After finding no one around to catch the slip, she continued, "I mean tenants. It's important you know my family history. My grandmother was one of the earliest investors in Mayview. Even before ground broke, she bought a chunk of the units from the development company. And then during construction, she saw huge potential in the area and the trend in malls out west, so she bought even more units. Gammy became a major investor in this place, then eventually negotiated to buy the rights to the whole damn thing."

"Gammy sounds like a helluva woman."

"It gets better. Before she passed away a few years ago, she transferred all ownership to her children. My mom and uncle Rob. With one stipulation: the mall stays within the family."

I scratched my chin, losing my train of thought after catching a glance of Debbie sweeping inside the store. "I uh... I think I'm picking up why you're telling me." The bookseller stopped to lean her broom like a mic stand, singing to whatever jazzy tune was playing overheard.

Tiffany caught my wandering eyes and sidestepped to block the performance. "Good. I'm hoping you're smarter than the stupid look on your face. My mom's sick. It's not looking good."

Her words snapped me back to attention. "I'm really sorry to hear that." I could empathize—my mom had just gone through a long ordeal herself and thankfully pulled through. She was a fighter, like her stubborn son. Or maybe it was the other way around.

"Thanks. I take it you've already met my sister, right?" She turned to point at the cute goofball dancing in the bookstore. "We haven't always seen eye to eye, but we definitely disagree with our uncle. He's been scheming to sell the mall even before mom got sick. And now that Deb and I stand to get mom's fifty percent, he's been offering to buy us out. The weasel is persistent. Sure does make a tempting offer." Before I could process any of the last words, Tiffany pulled at my shoulder. "Speak of the devil, here he comes."

I craned my neck to see the movie villain himself. Impatiently checking his watch while the escalator powered him up, I confirmed the pony-tailed hothead and Rob were one and the same.

"I can't wait to meet him," I said under my breath.

"Remember, nobody knows about our arrangement. To him, you're just overseeing the typical security duties." She finished as her uncle entered earshot, welcoming him with a fake smile. "Hey Uncle Rob, glad you got the message. I know you're busy, here's—"

"It's a mess, Tiff! The froyo place is on the fritz again!" Even through the suit I clocked tense muscles in the man's shoulders. "*This* the new security guy you hired?"

By the sound of it, I had another fan. And from his folded arms and deep squint, the looks of it too.

"Paul Washington." I extended a hand. "Nice to meet you."

To my surprise he returned the shake, but not after a lengthy pause.

He turned to Tiffany after adjusting his clip-on tie. "You really should have run this by me. This place isn't doing so hot, you know?"

"Uncle Rob!" The niece was none too pleased after being upstaged in front of her new employee. I got the impression that it was more than an act. To be fair, this guy radiated all kinds of jerk—and he was climbing the suspect list fast.

"Seriously Tiff. We're running a business." The jet black ponytail whipped over as his eyes darted to the new guy.

"I've heard a lot about you, sir." I leaned into my former acting chops, channeling a bit of Deputy Dewey from *Scream*. "I'm excited to be working for you here at Mayview. I hear you're quite the businessman. I'd love to learn from you. That is, when I'm not busy keeping us safe and secure."

Did he just smile?

"See? This guy gets it." Robert was easy to read. And easier to charm. "Yeah kid, keep up the good work and maybe you'll be doing more than guarding malls for a living." He poked a thumb at his niece. "Tell this one that she needs to get into the twenty-first century and level this place. The city is interested in buying us out."

Not that I thought she was lying, but I didn't think I'd confirm Tiffany's story within seconds of meeting the guy. Uncle Robbie was loose-lipped and brash. And from the darting eyes and constant dinging of his phone, he was pulled in too many directions.

"Of course sir," I added with a smile that was more painful than the hangnail on my middle finger. "I'm ready for the future, whatever that looks like."

Rob cupped his extra wrinkly white hand on my shoulder with a few patronizing pats and started to raise his phone to an ear. "This guy's got potential. He can stay for now. Call me if anything blows up."

And just like that, he stalked away toward Macy's, yelling in a Slavic tongue at the unlucky recipient of his call.

"Well, that's the best introduction I can do," Tiffany said. "Hope you got a good idea of my dear old Uncle Rob. If you need to get in touch with him again, please call me. I have some ideas so you don't blow your cover."

I nodded. In this business, guys like Rob were a dime a dozen. "Thanks for filling me in. Any other surprises? Or people in the building around the time of the pickup, or have access to the security office?"

She shook her head and motioned to follow. I glanced back at the dancing queen before complying. So, my mousey crush owned more than the bookstore. This was getting interesting.

ON THE WAY to her office, Tiffany took a detour, landing us where my workday began.

"Hey Mrs. Cunningham, your usual nightcap?" said the young barista.

The mall owner nodded and turned to read me in silence, taking the liberty of guessing my usual poison. "And a green tea for the officer."

Not bad. I loved my coffee, but not at night. Although she didn't have me figured out as well as she thought. "Close, but no cigar. Make it iced. Add in a danish, too."

The barista nodded and zipped into action, likely his last order of the night. The mall would be closed in less than half an hour, and most of the employees were already standing outside their stores. Several performed haphazard stretches, clearly bored while the seconds ticked away. Others began pulling in their external displays and sandwich boards, securing them behind heavy metal grates. Tiffany found a freshly washed table and invited me by kicking out the opposing chair.

"So," she started. "What are your thoughts after your first day?"

"Quite the interesting family you have."

I waited while she thanked the barista for the giant frosty cup, overflowing with more sugar than coffee. My pastry and tea came next, just as big and just as free. Hanging with the owner had its perks. I bit into the danish, finding it harder than something from the Easy-Bake oven we had on set of my sitcom. My co-star, Jenna Cooper, used to lug that thing around from her trailer. Last I heard, she wasn't doing so hot, making me one of the few childhood actors thriving—solving mysteries instead of struggling.

Tiffany watched my reaction to the bite, then continued, "*Interesting* is one word for us."

"None of what you told me is public. I did a deep dive before we met."

"I had hoped you would." She leaned forward and wrapped her lips around the straw, taking a lengthy, exaggerated pull while she peered into my soul. After downing half the drink, she wiped her lips and traced the rim of the cup. "Like I said, I respect you wanting to make up your own mind about the cast here, but I'm on a timeline. And my husband is pressuring me to call the police sooner."

I focused on each word carefully—a flicker of disdain when mentioning her husband. Like our first meeting, she was laying on that vampiric charm. Or was she just that into flirting? Either way, I needed to know more about her other half. Everyone was fair game.

"What's his take on the theft?"

"Theft. I hate the word but keep hearing it. I still can't believe it's come to this," she sighed and inhaled another quarter of the pseudo-coffee, this time no seduction. "He wants me to cut our losses and sell. Hates seeing me stressed. What partner would?"

I let the silence linger. Interpersonal conflict was my wheelhouse. People tend to talk when you let them—or make them uncomfortable.

Her forehead rippled a deep sea of wrinkles. "What? You think he has something to do with this?"

After a swig of icy matcha, I leaned back, way too comfortably —not responding.

"He's been nothing but supportive," she added. "Wyatt is just sick of owning a business. Specifically this one."

So the husband is not *that* supportive, check. "You didn't seem too keen on him when you were playing verbal footsie with me yesterday, ma'am."

The rest of her drink disappeared, followed by a long, drawn out lick across her wine colored lips. "So presumptive. Not every relationship is monogamous, detective."

"I don't mix business and pleasure," I said, as deadpan as I could muster.

"Again, there you go assuming things," she said with a coy smile.

Tiffany sure was confusing. I wished Geri could see this. I changed the subject. "I had no idea Debbie was your sister."

She chuckled, acknowledging the abrupt lane change. "I'll give you a pass on that, *detective*. She's my half sister. Her dad is Puerto Rican. I wish I could have her glow. My tanning bed barely cuts it." She extended her arms, studying her complexion.

"You guys get along?"

"Well enough. We both want to keep the mall alive, despite what Uncle Rob thinks. I won't lie, there were issues at first. Mom's will guarantees us an equal split, but all Deb wanted was that one little bookstore. I couldn't fathom why she handed over the whole mall and got paranoid that she'd screw me over. I ran with it though, jumped at the chance to run the place. Well, along with my uncle. Now I understand why. The work here is never ending."

After a poorly received comment comparing the mall to a game of SimCity, I got the conversation back on track. "She doesn't share in the mall's profits?"

"Legally, Deb could ask for her cut, but she never has. She only keeps what the bookstore makes. And of course there's free rent. Otherwise she stays cooped in that little shop. I suppose that's fair, but I've always had a weird sense she's not telling me something.

Although lately she's stepped up, scheduling events and helping with marketing. My uncle, not so much."

Debbie didn't sound like someone chasing the money. Relief washed over as the sister dropped down a slot on the suspect list.

A trio of bracelets jangled as Tiffany spied a message on her smartwatch. "That's my cue," she said after a chortle. "Before I go, I decided to take you up on your offer from this morning. I spoke to all the tenants who still prefer cash and made sure I was loud about it. Oh, and it's happening *tonight*. They have already started leaving their payments in the drop box outside my office. A few wanted to hand them over like usual, but I made excuses to force the drop."

Wow. Earlier today, Tiffany was a hard no for my wild plan. I didn't blame her. It was risky, poorly thought out, and had tons of room to go off the tracks. Marinating on it must have done the trick. My idea... my hope: force our crook into action by making the jackpot too alluring to resist. And urgency makes for mistakes.

She cracked her neck and sighed. "I'll be honest, I'm nervous. All that money… it will be an easy target for the thief. I'm going to go count what's already there before I head home. You can start your surveillance then. And I'll be back around six to collect the rest and then I'll head to the bank, assuming it's there. If any funny business is going to happen, it'll be in the next few hours. Good luck."

With all a go, tonight, I would catch them in the act. The part I was *not* looking forward to was the last-minute stakeout. When I proposed the idea this morning, I wasn't imagining it would happen without notice. Sitting for hours on end was a typical part of my job and something I've gotten used to—but I always had plenty of time to prepare. My meal, what I drank, getting in some exercise—if I was going to sit in place until the sun came up, I had to be as sharp as possible. I didn't like being thrown off my game.

"Thanks for the heads up," I said dryly as she stood. "And here I thought you'd want to have a slumber party."

"I've seen those movies. They don't end well. Enjoy." She

motioned to the counter and the steaming cup of coffee waiting. At least there was that.

"Oh." She looked over her shoulder. "Bart's pulling a double too. I told him to cover the outside. Between the two of you, let's hope you can figure this out. Don't screw this up."

And just like that, my childhood dream of being alone in the mall began. Until the nightmare, that is.

Chapter 8

"ATTENTION MALL SHOPPERS!" Debbie's voice sang from the speaker above. "The mall is now officially closed. You don't have to go home, but you can't stay here. We'll be waiting for you, bright and early tomorrow at nine o'clock, on the dot!"

Bart gave me a nod. "This is it, boss." He stood and handed me a walkie. "Channel 2 if you need anything. I'll be patrolling outside in the Jeep."

"Check in every half hour. And if you see anything out of the ordinary, call right away."

The young guard nodded again, then headed into the darkened parking lot, full of confidence and a sugary energy drink. Behind him, an elderly couple shuffled out, followed by the last visitor, a mall walker with a healthy sheen of sweat from the vigorous evening jaunt. After a final look, I confirmed I was the only one left and locked the doors.

Soon, I'd be recreating my favorite scenes from the nineties flick *Career Opportunities*. In the coming of age movie, a newly hired night cleanup boy is left alone in a department store to live out all sorts of goofiness. Of course, he's interrupted by a pair of burglars, foiling the fun with a robbery at gunpoint. Our hero eventually survives the night, even leaving with a new found soulmate. I imagined Debbie in the Jennifer Connolly role until I absentmindedly walked into a garbage can, narrowly catching myself as I tumbled onto a bench.

As if from my daydream, her voice boomed from above. "I hope you're better at security than you are walking!"

Normally, I wouldn't be embarrassed. But getting caught on candid camera by my crush knocked me off my game—for the second time tonight. I dusted off and beamed a smile at the first camera in sight, then headed towards the security office. Hopefully I could catch the cutie before she went home.

A loud echo bounced off the walls with each step toward the center of the mall. As I drew closer to the escalator, a series of lights overhead dimmed, forcing my vision to rely on slivers of moonlight. Pressing on, the next group of LEDs faded, as if my presence brought on an impending darkness. Or *someone* was having fun controlling the lights at my expense. Lightly humming the New Kids hit, "Step by Step", I played it smooth, with every little step I took.

Finally reaching the *Employee Only* door, I felt a rush of nostalgia, remembering the childhood stories I made about what lay behind. With a quick swipe of a badge, the door opened, revealing the boring corridors—not the secret villain hideout or military complex from youthful daydreams.

The hallway carried the sounds of employees excitedly filing toward the staff parking lot exit.

"You guys heading over to Blake's?" I overheard a woman in her early twenties ask.

"You know it," one man replied. "Best apple cider in town."

As the group drew closer, I caught a glimpse of the white woman's multiple facial piercings, along with the dark work shirt hanging off her shoulder. No doubt the Gen Zer worked at my favorite highschool-era raver clothing store. Did I catch a bit of pink Manic Panic streaked on her locks? *Some things never change,* I thought to myself with a smile.

Before passing, the trendy woman shot an annoyed glance, as if to say, "who's the old guy?" Both her friends laughed on their way out, the buff Asian guy's chuckle booming. I could have sworn the scrawny white kid muttered something about Paul Blart. If I were their age, I'm sure I would have done the same—although I'd probably change the insult to Inspector Clouseau.

As I approached, the door to the security office swung open, nearly grazing my shoulder. Inside the dimly lit room, Debbie waited with arms crossed, tapping her foot like Sonic the Hedgehog when you left the game running too long without hitting pause.

"Took you long enough," she said with a grin. "I'm a bigger fan of the Backstreet Boys, myself."

"Too much *TRL* for you." I assumed she was obsessed with the Carson Daly MTV show like most kids of the 90s. "I had a feeling someone was watching me. Having fun with the lights?"

Her shoulders relaxed as she shifted her weight onto the sole of a single converse. Chucky Ts, classic. I took notice of her wardrobe change—trading the black apron for distorted stonewash overalls on top of a long sleeve Blockbuster shirt. Her hair flowed freely, no longer tethered by multicolored bands in a ponytail. Unlike her sister, this girl knew the Death Star trench run straight to my heart.

She chuckled and walked to the computer. "I figured I'd show you the controls before starting inventory. Tiff told me you're pulling an all-nighter."

"Yeah?" I kept it vague. The boss said nobody else knew the real deal. What did she tell her sister?

"Yeah." She looked disappointed. "Something about a new shipment of massage chairs. Coming in straight from Korea and she didn't want them stuck at the Canadian border all night. Not sure it's the best investment, especially seeing as she suddenly needed rent earlier from the tenants. But it's nice to see her take more interest in improving the mall. I've been waiting for her to come around and have been begging her to renovate. While keeping the retro vibe, of course!"

I took a seat next to my favorite mall owner, catching the scent of lavender and bookstore. "Your sister not a big fan of the mall?"

She laughed, wiping her glasses across a pant leg before placing them back on her nose. Debbie's eyes sparkled, reflecting a faint lamp in the thick lenses covering the hazel gems. "Sometimes I wonder. Doesn't seem like it sometimes. She definitely doesn't nerd out like I do." She paused slightly, cocking her head to look into my eyes. "Like we do."

Interesting. Tiffany had made it sound like she was all-in on the mall, with her little sister just beginning to care. But the nerdy girl in front of me was more than a fair weather fan. I realized I was blushing. Some detective I was—I couldn't keep my cool near her. I really needed a chat with my neighbor after today. *Why the hell did Geri go out of town now?*

"I've read your articles." She chuckled. "I'd be lying if I said I didn't shed a few tears over your Family Video piece. It's what landed you the gig here. I guess you have me to thank."

My eyes narrowed. "Oh, is that so?"

"Yeah. Tiffy asked if I knew about the retro obsessed private eye. I didn't think she'd actually call you. Or you'd take the offer to work here."

She recommended *me*? Another wrinkle in the case. From the way things were looking, this smelled like an inside job—with family at the top of the list. But Debbie? *She couldn't have been the thief, could she?* It was probably a good thing the stakeout was tonight, only having a few days before Tiffany calls in Detroit's Finest.

I chuckled to myself, making an obvious connection all too late. "Deborah… Debbie Gibson. Tiffany. Your mom was really into malls, I take it?"

"Very smart, detective," she smiled. "Tiffany was actually named before the mall singer fad, but mom liked the theme and ran with it when I was born. Personally, I'm a bigger fan of Selena, but what can you do? "

"I learned about your family. Grandma was quite ambitious. What about your dads?"

"Hah. You reminded me of that show, *My Two Dads*." She snorted a laugh. "Tiff's dad passed away a while ago. And my dad has been in Puerto Rico for over a decade now. Mom and dad were never that close." She put her fingers together to make a hand-heart. "Product of some *summer lovin'*, had them some fun."

I hadn't met anyone else that could fit more pop culture references in a single interaction than my friend Corey. And he had an excuse, owning a pawn shop and all.

"Alright then," I started. "Since we're going to be working together, any plot twists you think I should know about? Strange dealings, suspicious people, children living in the walls?"

"My uncle's been extra stressed the past few weeks. You might want to steer clear of him. The way his forehead vein is bulging out, I can tell something is gnawing on him. And he's been harping us to sell this place harder than usual."

She leaned back in the chair, scanning the wall of security cameras. A slender, unmanicured index finger pointed to one of the screens. "See, there he is now. Just look at the way he walks. So frantic, like that scene in the second *Problem Child* movie when the teacher is running to the bathroom."

I nodded with a slight smile, fighting the urge to name the actor. "Is he normally here this late?"

"Nada, señor," she rolled the *r* heavily. It sounded natural.

And there we had it. All signs pointed to the angry man. Uncle Rob chipping money off the top for himself. He nets the extra cash while adding pressure on the girls to sell, forcing them to join his plan to break Gamma's promise. Motive, check.

A buzz tickled my pocket. I glanced at my phone, catching the text from Corey.

> Got another one of these packages. Stop by the shop when you can.

I shook my head and rehomed the cell. Another mystery that would have to wait.

"Busy guy," she said, spinning the chair to face the screens. "I have to head out in a minute anyway, so let me show you all the doo-dads."

Deb spent the next five minutes giving a tutorial of the security system. I wondered why Bart wasn't my teacher until I realized she was doing both of us a favor. She was quick, detailed, and enthusiastic. I learned how to operate the lights, the security gates, and how to adjust the cameras. And, along with a reminder of the crash course from earlier, the PA system.

"I heard you already know about the music controls," she smirked. "Just don't have too much fun here all alone." She stood, grabbing the boombox shaped purse I hadn't noticed on the counter.

"Sure you don't want to join me? Your sister turned down the offer to have a good ole fashioned lock-in." I immediately regretted the words and tried to course correct. "Like all night laser tag back in the day."

Squinted eyes peered back, solidifying the regret. "I was a bigger fan of roller skating lock-ins. And besides, it's date night. I doubt my boyfriend would like that." She winked. "But thanks for the offer, *dick*."

Somehow, I got the sense she wasn't referring to my profession. Great. I never knew when to keep my mouth shut. At least the case was ready to crack. Now to catch Uncle Robbie red handed. Hopefully he would hurry up—there was a pro-wrestling Pay-Per-View tonight, and if the rumor was true, Chris Jericho was announcing his retirement. But first, I had to wait out my boss until she left.

I spent the next hour wandering the gloomy, vacant halls, thoughts occasionally broken by a check in from Bart. Slow measured breaths and my own echoing footsteps were the only noises in the eerie dim light. As I slowly made my way from one wing to the next, I imagined the old stores that once filled each empty space. Decades ago, KayBee Toys used its magnetic force to draw me inside, the final destination on my hunt for a Catwoman action figure from *Batman Returns*. My mother, the saint, spending a full week hunting through toy aisles until we hit paydirt. Across the shiny white tiled floor, memories of another 90s struggle: spend my allowance at Babbage's on a new computer game, or visit FuncoLand for the latest sports cartridge. Near the edge of the corridor was another gated, empty shop. I laughed quietly, remembering the summer I got my ear pierced at Claire's, my agent being more angry than my mom. I remember overhearing the conversation, Baxter having to tell the writers of my character's new look before season 2. They were not happy—I wanted to rock the black metal stud that was all the rage.

It was no secret the mall held a special place in my heart. Especially this one. Despite my brushes with fame, my life began fairly normally—until I was whisked away to Cali partway through grade school. On the occasional visits back to Michigan, Mayview Mall felt more of a home then the hotels, or wherever dad was living at the time. It was a constant. It was always here. And then when we moved back permanently, the mall was that safe space where I could feel like a kid. And meet other kids. Sure, I tried going to school like a normal student. I even lasted two years at one of them until switching to a much smaller private academy. My choice—going from an overnight celebrity to just Paul was what you could guess—a blessing and a curse. I bounced between Mr. Popular and being teased. Even back then I realized it was a projection of teenaged jealousy, but it still sucked. After trial and error with the school system, the decision to learn at home was what worked out best. And going to the mall gave me what I missed.

I closed my eyes, drifting away, hearing and seeing the nineties —a packed shopping mall. Debbie walked by with a gaggle of girls, singing "Genie in a Bottle" as they passed. Her brown hair was secured in a high ponytail, held tight by a bright green ripply scrunchie. The equally glowing pink fanny pack covered part of the white Spice Girls shirt, emblazoned with the debut album cover. Faded denim shorts showed off the frayed hemming, more loose than anything you'd find today. A pair of translucent jelly shoes completed the look, making squishy noises with each footfall. The scent of cucumber melon body spray lingered like it was the group's calling card. Debbie looked back, eyes meeting mine while taking a long sip of her frozen cola. I instinctively searched my pockets for Binaca, realizing I hadn't used the minty mouth spray in decades.

The daydream morphed away leaving me alone in the darkness. *What grade would Debbie have been when I was a senior?* That was the true gauge of a relationship's success, right? I was an elder millennial, just on the cusp of Gen X. Debbie seemed like she was my equal in pop culture, but that youthful zest was so difficult to place. I sauntered on, remembering my focus, counting down the minutes until the real work began.

Chapter 9

"CHECKING IN, BOSS," Bart's voice crackled over the walkie. "Ten-thirty and the parking lot is empty, except for a few of the staff vehicles. And this cool *Back to the Future* car."

"Make sure you keep a close eye on that one," I joked. The car still ran great, but it was quite an ordeal finding a mechanic that understood the DMC DeLorean. "How many cars in total?" I flipped through the outdoor CCTV cameras, watching the blinking light on Bart's Jeep as it crept past Macy's.

"Other than ours, we have Robert's BMW. Mrs. Tiffany's BMW is also here. And.." I waited for him to finish, following the Jeep across the screen. "Ok, here is Debbie's cool little yellow Kia. And Hakim is walking to his car right now. Pretty late for him."

I watched Bart stop next to a shadow off screen, then resume his roll forward.

"Hakim was staying late to help with inventory. I stopped to say hi. Oh, and there's Forrest's pickup truck."

Bart launched into the backstory of Forrest and Clayton, referring to them as the hardest working janitors. From his description, Clayton was the man I saw getting chewed out by Robert on my first day. I learned he often carpooled with Forrest, also on the night shift, his bearded and much older counterpart, at least to Bart. The two reminded me of the cops in *Lethal Weapon*, Forrest taking on Danny Glover's role.

"Thanks Bart. Check back in thirty. I'm going to do a walk around soon."

I leaned back in the chair and kicked my legs onto the counter, careful not to press any buttons. Now to make sense of the night. I massaged my temples, channeling Phillip Marlowe—the classic hardboiled detective I had no business comparing myself to. My mind instantly dodged the case and went straight to Debbie. Didn't she have a date tonight? Was she dating Hakim? *Not relevant right now,* Paul, I said to the wall of flickering screens.

Who's still here? Tiffany made sense. She said she'd be here late, counting the cash, and her last message was to start the office stakeout at 11 sharp. The janitors normally left around one after polishing the floors, according to Bart. Tiffany was adamant they weren't suspects, but it couldn't hurt to see what the old men knew. And there was Uncle Rob. Somewhere. A bunch of cars, and nobody on my CCTV screens. *Some help these things are.* I cycled through the cameras and finally found an older black man scrubbing tables in a dining area. From Bart's description, I knew it was Clayton's partner in grime, Forrest. Besides my 4-wheeled sidekick, the only other sign of life was the light from Sleuths. I planted my boots on the dark purple carpet and headed towards the food court. Then I'd loop over to the bookstore, and finally check on Tiffany. And then the long stakeout would begin, hopefully catching Rob, wherever he was.

The moonlit walk under the skylights was serene. Knowing only a handful of us were here made my stroll that much more peaceful. My soul was filled with a calm, yet electric buzz. While the keycard and badge said otherwise, I still believed I shouldn't be here. Every corner looked different, now bathed in darkness and shadows. Tucked away under the escalators, the seating nooks appeared ominous, hiding the leather-wrapped sofas and little green plants—a unique, welcoming aesthetic of the mall in the daylight. I wondered if Geri would help me snatch and transport one of the fellas, a nice going away present after solving the case.

A soft hum trickled from the food court as I approached. The overhead lights were just as bright as the music was loud—the custodian was blasting P.M. Dawn from a small boombox set atop the Fast Wok counter. No free samples for me tonight. I chuckled, remembering the tradition of getting a complementary cube of orange chicken—the employees hoping to entice this passerby for a full order.

The grey bearded man swayed to the beat, rhythmically wiping down a table with a blue washcloth. Satisfied, he dunked the rag into soapy water, ready to rinse and repeat. "Baby, you send meee," Forrest sang to himself, bobbing his head, lost in the music. It was a jam, for sure.

I moved closer. With loud footfalls while clearing my throat, I hoped to avoid giving the man a startle. "Ahem. Great song. The original is a classic." The remake wasn't my favorite.

"You betcha, son." Forrest turned with a smile. "I heard you from a mile away." He looked a bit different in person, but cameras can do that sometimes, I guess.

"Good, I was trying not to scare you."

"Appreciate it, I really do. No need. Maybe the first few years workin' nights I'd have a shock or ten. Now, these ears are so finely tuned, I might as well double for security during these late nights. Although most of the time it's just birds or the mall ghosts."

I let out a small, disbelieving laugh. "Mall ghosts?"

He chuckled, then set the washrag down. "You know, the spirits. Crowley's. Montgomery Ward's. Lechmere." The crooked smile was disarming, stopping me in my tracks. Before I could press on, he continued. "Hah. I can see you don't believe."

Wrinkles formed on my forehead. "It's not that I don't believe. But things tend to have a rational explanation. Shaggy and Scooby always pulled a mask off to find the monster was an old white guy."

The man shook his head and bellowed a hearty laugh that

echoed off the beige walls. A long sigh escaped his mouth while a glint of light reflected from his dark eyes.

My eyes pinched into a squint. I knew I was funny, but his reaction was a shock.

He coughed and regained composure. "Ah, sorry, son. You're just so much like him. It's uncanny."

"We still talking about ghosts?" I asked.

"You don't remember me, do ya?"

I scratched an invisible itch on the back of my neck.

"Your dad used to bring you here all the time." The man chuckled again, staring past me into the darkened mall behind. "He was such a troublemaker when I first met him. Punk kid up to no good. Caught him with a can of spray paint behind the old Hudson's."

No way. I knew my dad worked at the mall, but he was the biggest rule follower I knew. Did this guy have me mixed up with someone else?

"He never told ya, huh? I made a deal with him. No cops if he worked a few weeks for me. Hard worker. Eventually got him a job at the old pretzel stand."

A gentle heat rushed into my cheeks. That part I knew. Dad loved telling tales about his summer exploits slinging pretzels. In my angsty anti-work teenage years, the Pretzel King stories were his big talking point to get my butt out of the house and collect a paycheck.

Forrest nodded, reliving a bit of his youth. "Hell, I even remember when he came back after graduating college. Told me he was gonna put that accounting degree to use and buy a store here. I was shocked when he showed up over a decade later with a cute little tyke. And a police badge."

He stopped, eyes returning to meet mine. "I'll bet you remember the free quarters for the arcade more than some old janitor."

That I did. "Quite the memory, sir."

He tapped his finger against a temple in the vein of iconic wrestling manager Bobby the Brain. "Still got it. At least the important stuff."

The trip down memory lane warmed my nostalgia loving heart. Dad a punk kid? And he dreamed of owning a shop in the mall? I would have to ask him next time I stopped by to get another box of childhood toys he keeps begging me to take.

While I'd determined the case all but solved, I wouldn't be one of Detroit's top P.I.'s if I didn't at least follow up on the task at hand. "Speaking of important stuff." I jumped in, using the natural segue. "Notice anything strange over the past month or two. Ghosts aside?"

The janitor furrowed his brow. "Now that you mention it, the owners have been on edge. Even more than usual. I can sense their stress. Robert has been even pushier and Tiffany, well, she's always changing her mind about this or that. Poor Deborah. How she's related to them, some days I can't understand."

"Robert's been pushier? How so?"

"He has been trying to sell this place for years. Tried to get the janitors here to help convince those girls to sell."

I thought of my first introduction to Robert, yelling at an unassuming Clayton. "He seems to be an angry guy, from what I've seen."

"Saw one of his outbursts, did you? There's always something. I ignore him. I guess it's easy to take out your frustrations on us old janitors."

"You've been here a while. You like working for them?"

"Like's a strong word." He took the washrag and started back on the table. "I owe that family everything, though. As long as they need me, I'll be here. And if you need anything, other than some quarters, let me know."

I returned his fist bump and made an about-face toward the bookstore, hoping to find Debbie. Forrest confirmed what I already knew: Uncle Robbie was dead set on offloading the mall and pressure was ramping up. The rest of the peaceful moonlit walk was uneventful, aside from a few whistles of wind I imagined were spirits.

A clean scent lingered in the air, mixed with the unmistakable smell I referred to as retail: Cinnabon, pretzel dough, and the plastic of new electronics. The dark, aromatic stroll became even darker, finding no light coming from the bookstore and the security gate closed tight. I must have just missed her. Dang. I switched gears again, ready to catch Tiffany before beginning my long stakeout of the manager's office.

Chapter 10

AFTER THE THIRD set of knocks and a few tries at the door, I was sure the manager's office was empty and locked tight. Perfect timing. Both sisters snuck out under my nose.

"Bart reporting in!" the walkie crackled with some serious static.

"Report in, Bart. How are things looking out there?"

"Beautiful night for a drive, boss. I've never done one of these overnights, but it's kinda relaxing. Getting a little sleepy, though."

"Great to hear. Well not the sleepy part. How's the parking lot?"

"Oh, let's see. Miss Debbie's yellow car is still here. Mrs. Tiffany just pulled away a few minutes ago. I see Forrest heading to his truck as we speak. No Clayton, maybe he left with someone else. It looks like it's just Miss Debbie, Robert, and us."

So the uncle was still lurking around. And where was Deb? I headed out of the corridor leading to the food court. A pleasant, lemony-fresh cleaning solution attacked my nostrils. I briefly floated to summers of hounding my neighbors to buy powdery Country-Time lemonade. Back in the real world, the place looked spotless. Hard working indeed—this place was lucky to have the old guy.

"Alright, Bart. Same drill. Check back in thirty, earlier if anything comes up."

Silence.

Unlike the kid not to respond right away, I thought to myself. I took a seat in the dining area, positing myself with a good view of the hall while waiting for a response.

Finally, after three minutes, the walkie clicked on. "Hey boss, it's Bart."

Of course it was. "You alright out there?"

"Yeah, sorry. Julie's out here. She works at Hot Topic and says she thinks she left her phone there." I heard a woman's voice mumbling underneath static. "What should I do?"

I leaned forward, elbows on the still-wet table. The Casio showed it was just after eleven. Should I help the girl out? Tiffany's office was locked tight. Cameras were all working. Bart had the outside lot covered. The only way in or out of that office had eyes on it for hours, aside from the emergency exit. And from my test earlier, I'd hear if that door opened over a mile away. My ears still had a little ring in them.

"Hold on." I took a quick stroll around the dining area, sizing up every vantage point and angle. Hopefully this wasn't a rookie mistake. "Ok Bart. Park at the food court entrance. Make sure you have a good view of the hallway to Tiffany's office."

"Aye Aye captain!"

"Tell her to meet me at the main Penney's entrance. She's got ten minutes."

Greeted by pale white prayer hands, I found they belonged to the punky woman I had seen leaving earlier. "Thank you, thank you, thank you!" She ran past the doors, causing me to hurry and lock them behind. "I've been looking for hours and realized I must have left my phone here!"

"Let's make it quick."

"Yes of course! It's really important." She raced forward, feet matching her rapid speech. "My dad left for Europe and I wanted to check on him to make sure he landed okay. And I don't work tomorrow."

Other than the business end of things, losing my phone would be a luxury. But not for the twenty-something, who knew nothing of T9 texting. I imagined myself in her shoes, figuring she had good reason to worry. "Let's find that phone and get you back on your way."

We marched through the quiet, desolate mall in silence, other than the clacks of our footwear and elevated breathing. Even though the woman was unassuming and smaller than me, I was on alert. The middle of the dark, empty mall was the perfect setting for a horror movie. Or a psychological thriller. And the timing of this little adventure seemed too much of a coincidence. I let her lead, eyes on her hands, watching for any sudden movements. But what would I do? I hadn't carried a weapon in years and my weekly visit to the dojo was purely cardio. My karate skills needed a true reboot, and I didn't mean a binge of *Cobra Kai*.

The stupidity of this started to sink in as we passed the mall fountain, now off, giving the smell of stale sitting water.

"Almost there!" she said excitedly, speeding up as she raced up the frozen escalator, two to three steps at a time.

Though nearly twice her age, this forty year old managed a decent job keeping pace with the young woman. She suddenly stopped in front of the white wall, turning to face me. "Could you open it? I don't have the keys." It took an extra second to register it as an employee entrance.

Great. If I didn't remember the pink and black-haired girl from earlier tonight, I would have believed this was a trap. Like a background character, fooled in an *Ocean's* something-or-other heist. They always made the guards look like dummies, and that was the last thing I needed for my career.

I pushed away newspaper headlines heralding my demise and hesitantly slid the keycard over the reader. A soft click unlocked the unassuming door hidden in the wall. I held it open for her to go first.

"Thanks!" She beamed her pearly whites, bubbling with too much energy for this time of night.

She scurried to the back entrance of her store, again waiting for me to open it. If she noticed my apprehension, she didn't let it show. She seemed disturbed, tapping her pockets, likely on autopilot, searching for her missing cell phone. Like looking for a pair of sunglasses sitting on your head. Some habits are hard to break.

Julie ran into the store first, leaving me in her dust. Instantly she squealed in delight, holding up the silver rectangle of her desires. "Thank goodness!" she exclaimed, grabbing the phone and flicking through notifications as if she were alone in the store.

I cleared my throat loudly. "You ready?"

"Oh sorry, I had some missed calls!" She shrugged and walked into the employee hallway, eyes fixed on her phone while nearly bumping into the wall. "Oops!"

She didn't learn the lesson, still glued to the device. After tripping over her feet, she finally pocketed the distraction—not without showing obvious signs of nervousness, fighting an urge to check the screen. Our trek out was slower, urgency gone now that her little lifeline was stowed away safely.

Annoyance got the best of me—the whole ordeal took less than seven minutes and broke the monotony of a stakeout, but I'd rather get back to work. Thankfully, I was able to keep an eye on the food court for part of the endeavor while Bart kept a lookout from his car.

"You know," I started. "The sooner you're outta here, the sooner you can look at that phone."

She shot an uneasy smile and nodded, picking up the pace while we backtracked through the mall, ending back where we started. As the door behind her locked shut, the overnight security lighting flickered. More than once.

"Boss," Bart's voice buzzed through the walkie. "Looks like we're getting another power surge. Mall lights are on the fritz again."

In my line of work, things are rarely a coincidence.

Chapter 11

"KEEP WATCH FOR ANY FUNNY BUSINESS," I belted into the walkie while bursting into a brisk jog. "Eyes on that hallway! And listen for the emergency exit, just in case!"

Time to catch the culprit in the act. The soles of my sneakers pounded the smooth concrete floors bringing me closer to the manager's office. This was the part of the plan I didn't think through. What happens when I catch the crook? The jog turned into more of a hustle, and not the kind I danced during "My Eyes Don't Cry" at weddings.

I crept toward the food court, only finding Forrest's spotless attention to detail and not a soul in sight. In the distance, the hall leading to Tiffany's office was dark and eerily quiet.

"That you boss?" Bart's voice squeaked over the line.

"Yup, it's—"

The dim dining area lighting flickered again. I imagined a generator starting or stopping somewhere deep in the belly of the mall.

"Boss!"

"Yeah I see it, Bart," I said, inching closer to the corridor. "I got this area covered, resume your patrol and make sure no new challengers have arrived... or left"

After explaining the reference, I paused, briefly reflecting on the job. My stakeouts had a simple formula: chilling in a car, eating junk food, listening to the SiriusXM eighties on eight—and, of course, snapping pictures of torrid love affairs. Or at least adulterers walking into motel rooms and the occasional upscale Detroit casino. But this case was different. And with big money involved, things could get messy. *"Get it together, Paul,"* I whispered.

I was here to ID the crook, not apprehend them. While every kid dreams of being a masked vigilante at some point, I was no kid. This millennial body had no weapons, laughable formal training, and was all alone in a mall after midnight. Paid well, sure, but that wasn't enough to blow my first big case by trying to be a hero. I swallowed my pride to make space for logic and slithered away from the hallway, posting up underneath the counter of Fast Wok. With a great view of the hallway, nobody was getting in or out without me knowing. Hiding under the counter felt comfortable, a familiar feeling. Hidden surveillance like the guys undercover on *The Wire*—although they didn't have to deal with grease stuck to the walls.

A few long minutes of eerie nothingness passed. I wondered if I should have left Bart to watch while I checked the security office instead. Would I have found someone tampering with the cameras?

And then… footsteps.

This is it. Look alive, Paul. The most exciting—hell, the only exciting part of any stakeout.

"Hello?" A voice echoed from the distance. My spine tightened as I sank further toward the sticky kitchen floor. "Hello?" This time, I recognized the voice: Debbie. What was she doing here? Last I checked, her store had closed hours ago.

More knocking rapped further away—my sleep deprived brain heard the rhythmic beating of Bel Biv DeVoe's song, "Poison".

"Tiffany?" Debbie said, followed by more knocking. I placed the noise coming from the hallway. "You in there?"

Was I wrong? Was Debbie about to steal the cash? Everything pointed to Uncle Robbie. But maybe I'd let my guard down too low, falling for the spunky girl. I had to get a closer look.

A peek around the corner all but confirmed my suspicions—

Tiffany's sister stood in front of the door wearing a confused look while she tapped at her phone.

I did *Da' Dip*, just out of view, and listened to the call.

"Hey, Tiff. Sorry I missed your text. I was finishing inventory. I'm at your office now and nobody's here. Is everything okay? Call me. I'm heading out in a few minutes." She sounded concerned, not what I'd expect from a thief. But I've been wrong before, if you can believe that. "What is going on?" the brunette whispered.

What was going on indeed.

If she *was* the thief, this would be the perfect chance to sneak in and pilfer through the safe. Instead, I heard the squeak of her sneakers while she turned to head back—toward me.

"I thought you left," I said, casually popping out from the corner.

The store owner jumped, clutching her chest as a high-pitched peep escaped her mouth. "What the hell!"

I walked closer to meet her at the end of the hall. "Sorry," I said, trying to hold back a smile. "What about that hot date with your boyfriend?"

Her arms folded over. "Every other Friday is inventory night. Gives me time to check in with my boys, like Poirot or Hammer or Marlowe."

I failed to hide a different kind of smile. "Why are you sneaking around here?"

"Sneaking? I don't care much for that tone." She shook her head. "Here one day and you're already on my case. Figures Tiffany has it out for me."

She blew past, powering away, heavy footfalls and a gait with purpose.

"Hey!" I jogged beside to match her pace. "I'm just doing what I'm told. It's around midnight and I didn't expect to see you here."

She stopped and turned to study my expression, tilting her head back and forth. Those shiny hazel eyes pulled me in, glowing with the hazy moonlight from the skylights.

"You sound sincere. You do," she said. "But our family has issues, if you haven't noticed. Things aren't as friendly as they seem, but it's really none of your business. Sorry you're caught in the crossfire."

Oh, but it was my business. I just couldn't tell her that.

I raised my palms up slowly. "Speaking only as the security guy, I swear. I'm just wondering, why did you stop by the office? It sounded like you were looking for someone?"

"I am. Inventory usually takes me a while. Mostly because I'll knock over a book and start reading, and by the time I know it, it's two in the morning and I haven't even started looking at the stock."

"I don't follow."

"Getting there, gumshoe. I was deep in the pages, as usual. Lost in a story I've read at least a dozen times. And then the lights start flickering, zapping me back to reality."

"That happen often?" I interrupted.

"Oh yeah. If my feet aren't firmly planted on the ground, my face is in a movie or book. Otherwise, I'm floating through the information superhighway in my own head."

I laughed. "Not what I mean."

"Oh." Her eyes darted away. "You meant the lights, didn't you? Yeah, that's been happening more these days. Every so often, usually around night."

"Interesting. So, you were zapped..."

"Right. I got back on track, logging the latest shipment of books until I glanced at my phone. I keep it on silent most of the time. Helps me avoid distractions. It also means I miss pretty much everything. Like a text from Tiff to come see her ASAP."

"Is that… normal?" I asked, my voice laced with doubt.

"Is something weird going on around here? You *really do* sound like more of a gumshoe than mall security!"

I got my answers, but it was clear it came at a cost. If she hadn't already, she was close to seeing through my little act. Time to recover.

"Oh yeah," I said without much emotion. "Must be me slipping into old habits. I wanted to make sure I understand as much as I can around here. I'm a stickler for safety. Why didn't you go inside the office?"

"Ha! You think Tiffany would give me a key?"

"You are her sister."

"Exactly. She keeps me far away from mall business. Like I said earlier, I finally got her on board to let me run some events to drum up traffic. Would you believe I haven't been inside her office in weeks? Not sure what she wanted tonight. "

"Well then. I feel like I wouldn't be doing my job now if we at least didn't follow up." I held out an index finger, a tiny keyring dangling off the tip. "Care to join me?"

Debbie followed me to the office, mumbling something about a stranger having more access than her. Even after the strange encounter with my current crush, Uncle Robbie was still suspect number one. Debbie seemed too genuine and kept her story straight, but I couldn't completely scratch her off the list, biases and all.

"Alright." I inserted the key, building the suspense. "Let's see what's going on in here."

Chapter 12

THE DOOR CREAKED OPEN. Lights still on, the office was just as I remembered, except for a few pages scattered on the desk and the scent of bourbon bombarding my nostrils.

"Damn." Debbie coughed from behind. "Uncle Robbie musta stopped by. Look, he left his calling card." She pointed to the empty bottle of whiskey in the trash can.

"Where is your uncle, anyway? His car is still out there."

"Hmm. Tiffany's obviously not here." Debbie paced the tiny room, then sifted through the papers. "I suppose it's relevant to your job." Her face scrunched up for a moment before continuing. "Sometimes Uncle Robbie has too much to drink and falls asleep somewhere around here after we close. I was hoping I wouldn't have to mention it. It used to be once in a blue moon. Lately it's been happening more. He's probably in the maintenance room dozing off or watching TV."

"Maintenance room? That wasn't part of the grand tour. Where's that?"

"The door next to the sports store. It's super easy to miss. Stairs will take you down there. Creepy boilers and mechanical stuff." She smirked. "This mall is filled with more secret passageways than a creepy old mansion on the hills. I kind of love it. Until you hear odd noises when you're supposed to be alone."

"Care to show me?" I flashed puppy dog eyes, which she didn't even notice.

"No thanks, I'd rather go home and watch *Clue* to get my fix. I really should get going. I'm opening the store in less than..." She paused to look at a multicolored Rainbow Brite watch, "Ugh. Eight hours. Why did Hakim have to go out of town this weekend?"

"Aww," I said, with my lower lip protruding in a pouty expression. I seemed back on her good side, or at least enough to be playful. "How's about I walk you out, miss?"

Her shrug turned into a *"Sure, why not."*

I radioed for Bart to cover the area once more, waiting for his "I'm in position, boss" before I walked the bookish beauty out.

Our stroll through the shadowy mall was uneventful, other than learning she had a childhood crush on Corey Feldman. After trading quotes from *The Goonies* and *License to Drive,* we said our goodbyes, leaving on a positive note. The change in tone left the impression she looked forward to seeing me again—a stark change from how the night began.

With only Robbie left, I figured finding my phantom of the mall was more important than the adventures in babysitting Tiffany's little room, especially now that my young cohort took over that duty. I scurried over to the security office, hoping to find any clues related to the mysterious power outages, or if I was lucky, find the whisky loving man on camera.

The employee hallway was dark and creepy, just like most of the building. No signs of life between the liminal voids, a feeling I still hadn't grown used to. The only time I'd seen a mall this empty was in the classic zombie movie, *Dawn of the Dead.* A thought that made every crack and creak sound like an undead shopper shambling out from the darkness.

"Compose yourself," I whispered out loud.

This job brought out a new side of me—a healthy sense of fear. It seemed for far too long, especially after the divorce, I had taken dumb risks that could have ended poorly. Sure, it helped my career, fearlessly sneaking around late at night to catch cheating partners. But leaping over private fences, tailing angry, gun-toting men, and even a night of train hopping was the very definition of foolish. But now, my mind was seeing caution signs, a foreign sensation that I wasn't ready to analyze—one more thing to save for Geri.

The soft, calming hum of equipment was the only noise in the security office. Tempted, I fought the urge to fire up the PA system and blast my latest obsession, vaporwave artist George Clanton. With my luck, I'd be jamming out to his latest album while I missed a robbery or found a body. *Need to keep my senses sharp for tonight.*

No signs of foul play—not that I knew what I was looking for. I glanced at the security monitors. Stillness of a cool night. Bart's Jeep idled in front of the food court entrance, his fuzzy head laser focused on the doors. Kid had a great attention to detail and was starting to grow on me. The other screens were just as dormant, filled with darkness only broken by a scattering of light posts in the parking lot—the ones that worked anyway. Poor mall was struggling. Working behind the scenes, it was worse than I thought. People were coming, sure, but it was a far cry from the heyday of my childhood. I couldn't imagine a time without this place, but if the girls' uncle had his way, that would soon be a reality.

I clicked on my walkie, watching Bart's Jeep on the screen. "Hey bud, how are things looking out there?"

The pixelated shape was anchored in place. "Hey boss. Looking good. Getting pretty quiet."

"Any activity near Tiffany's office?"

"No sir. I have a great view from the car. Even have the window open to listen for the alarm. I haven't seen anyone since you and Miss Debbie walked away. You like her, don't you?"

I ignored the question. "I'm at the security desk right now. How do I view the recordings of the last few hours?"

"We've been glued to that office all night, what are you looking for?"

"Good question. How would I know if anyone messed with this thing?"

The next five minutes of the young man's instructions made me wish for Debbie even more—purely for the explanation of the security system, of course. After clicking through a more dated program than the digital encyclopedia *Encarta,* it was painfully clear there was a problem.

"Wait." Bart perked up. "There's no files in that folder?

"That's what I said."

"Is the little red recording light on?"

"Green as a jolly giant. It actually says '*Not Armed*'."

"I got bad news for you, boss."

Without much help from the kid, I had determined that not only were the cameras no longer recording, but all footage from tonight was erased.

"Say," Bart chimed in. "I know this is bad timing but, you think I could come in for a bathroom break?"

How long had he been out there? I hoped he wasn't holding it. "I'll meet you in the food court. We need to regroup anyway. I've got a bad feeling."

My new sidekick must have raced into the building—he was already walking out of the restroom as I made my way over to greet him. We powered toward Tiffany's office, the walk just as quiet and uneventful as the last few hours we spent staring in its direction. Bart opened the door, just as shocked as Debbie had been by the lingering scent of bourbon.

"What are we looking for in here?" he asked. "You know we can't catch them in the act if we're in here!" The young guard looked around nervously.

"You know the code to the safe, don't you?"

Bart traced his toe on the ground while grimacing. "Mrs. Tiffany says I'm only supposed to open it in an emergency."

"Open it, Bart. Open it now."

The security officer played with the commercial-grade safe until it made a satisfying click and popped open to reveal...

Nothing.

Chapter 13

"HOW IS THIS POSSIBLE!" Bart sprang from the ground, a hand covering his face. "We've been watching ever since Mrs. Tiffany left!"

I took a deep breath, trying to channel my inner Van Damme while fighting thoughts of blowing the case, royally. "Another good question, padawan."

"And the cameras are out! Oh jeez, should we call the police? Mrs. Tiffany is gonna be livid!"

He was right. I had one job and I missed the mark. Maybe another P.I. would call his boss and tell her the jig was up. This one though? *Now* it's time for plan B. The stakeout was over. Time to swap out the stoic Jean Claude and tag in the one man wrecking crew. Or in this case, one and a half.

"We still have a chance, Bart. Robert's car is still out there, right?" The young man frantically nodded. "We need to check out that maintenance area."

"Why do you wanna go down there, boss?" Bart asked while we puttered our way past dozens of gated off stores, some permanently, some for the night. "It's kinda spooky."

"Didn't take you for someone that creeps out easy, Bart."

"Yeah, well, the mall is all fine and dandy in the daylight. But at night, there's stories this place is haunted."

"So I've heard. Mall ghosts, huh?"

"Yeah, something like that. But if this is what we gotta do, I got your back. And I mean it. You go in first." He extended a hand to the smooth brown door tucked between the sporting goods shop and an empty, gated up store that once sold candles.

"Thanks, I guess."

To my surprise, the same key for Tiffany's office unlocked the door—a skeleton key of sorts. Along the wall, a broken light switch forced us to rely on flashlights, more than bright enough to illuminate the way. Heat intensified as we cautiously moved forward in the cramped corridor, walls closing in the further we went. Using my free hand as a guide along the smooth, lacquered wall, the hall snaked around a corner. A faint light emanated from below, brighter with each step, allowing us to put our flashlights away.

"Watch your step," Bart said from behind.

After stumbling down the uneven, old concrete steps, I planted my feet firmly on the dusty floor. The giant open space was reminiscent of the boiler rooms I'd seen in some of the *Nightmare* films. Pipes of all shapes and sizes ran across the ceilings, twisting and branching away in every direction. The brown paint cracked walls were separated by rusty steel beams, looking like they'd lost their shine decades ago. In fact, everything was dull, grimy, and shaded black—not a fun neon color in sight—unlike my new office.

"Happy? You said you wanted to see the service tunnels." Bart's voice wavered. "That door on the right, that's the main control room. HVAC, water, backup electricity, that sort of thing. We don't normally go down here since we can control most of this from the security office."

"Who has access to this place?"

"Just us. Security I mean. Oh, and the cleaning crew. And I'm sure the owners do too, although I doubt they'd want to wander down here!"

So pretty much everyone, I thought.

The overhead steel shook and rattled violently, a loud rumble groaning from just a dozen feet away. I almost jumped out of my skin before realizing it was a boiler kicking on. After watching a stream of wispy air shoot from the leaky pipes, mildew and oil attacked my senses. The blast caused my eyes to water as the murky cloud drifted by.

Bart wheezed and began coughing, covering his mouth with the collar of his shirt. "We about done here, boss? I don't think anyone's down here."

"Almost, let's check out the room first."

I took Bart's cue and covered my face while hustling over to the door marked *'Authorized Personnel Only'*. Fingers ran over the bumpy door, pressing hard into someone's initials etched into the paint. The door gave way, opening to a workroom half the size of my apartment, and much less welcoming. Through the flickering fluorescent lights I saw workbenches lining the walls, most holding an assortment of tools: drills, hammers, and pieces of electrical equipment. Above, faded posters of Cindy Crawford and Kathy Ireland struggled to hang on the wall, duct tape proving its worth after a long battle with time. Further in the corner, a collection of stacked milk crates acted as a TV stand, holding an old CRT that would fetch a decent amount at my friend's pawn shop, assuming it still worked. I almost tripped over a glass bottle, sending it rolling across the yellow tiled floor. Thankfully it remained intact after slamming against the wall.

"You okay?" Bart asked, now at my side.

"Yeah, what was..."

I found the bottle, seeing it had landed near a twin sized cot—the kind you'd throw in a tent to make your camping trip a little more comfortable. On top, a comforter collected more empty bottles. Whisky, from the look of it. *Not to mention the familiar smell.*

"Pee-youuu!" I waved a hand near my nose, like it would do anything other than move some air in the tiny, stinky room.

"So it's true." Bart inched to the makeshift bed like he was approaching a velociraptor cage. "I've heard rumors but it sounded silly."

"Uncle Robbie taking his work home, I see. Or is it the other way around?" I stroked my chin, joining the young security officer at the edge of the room.

We searched the area for a minute, finding nothing noteworthy. Unless you count collecting recyclables, that is.

After another coughing fit and a noticeable change in posture, Bart again asked if we were done with the wild goose chase.

"Yeah, let's keep moving," I said. "At least this confirms that Robert's been hiding out down here. If his car is still outside, he's got to be somewhere close by."

"You got it." He paused, scanning the dusty living area. "After seeing this room, I get why I'd see his car when I'd finish a shift, and then again bright and early when I got in."

"I think we call that pulling a Costanza."

Through Bart's confused expression, I could tell he'd never seen an episode of *Seinfeld*. Youth of today, what a shame.

"He never left," I explained.

"Oh, sure." He nervously wrung his wrist, asking the question burning in both our minds: "Where the heck is he then?"

"Beats—"

The thump of steel on steel caused us both to jump, Bart's shoulder grazing into mine before he tumbled backward.

Chapter 14

"HEY! ANYONE BACK THERE?" the gruff voice fought over the sound of rumbling mechanical equipment.

Bart's head spun to me then back at the door before his shoulders dropped, followed by his neck muscles loosening. "Hey Mr. Clayton, it's me, Bart. And the new security director."

In the open doorway, I recognized the man Robert had grilled days before. With a noticeable limp, the heavier white man in his late-fifties sauntered in like a cowboy entering a saloon. The only thing missing was a pair of batwing doors to announce his entry. His blue jumpsuit reminded me more of a certain horror icon than a janitor. If Bart weren't with me, I'd have a feeling I'd be tuning up the band for a potential roundhouse kick.

"Bart." Clayton nodded, sending his long, frizzled light hair forward. "So you're the new guy, huh." It wasn't a question. The man continued his slow shuffle into the room, then dropped a toolbox on a workbench. Either the loud thump was unintentional, or the guy really needed some Hakuna Matata.

"Yes sir," I said, not acknowledging his sour look. "The names, Paul. I thought we were alone here."

Clayton leaned into the bench and crossed his arms. His face scrunched for a few seconds, a long squint studying the trespasser in what may have been his office. At least before Robbie took over.

"You're never alone down here. Welcome aboard," the custodian said, dropping the scowl while approaching with an open hand. The handshake was firm and greasy—to be expected from a hard day's work. "Had you going there, didn't I?" He smiled.

Bart guffawed from the corner, clearly amused by the tough guy act. In my defense, other than the Michael Meyers getup, my heart rate barely flinched. The surroundings were scary, sure, but after dealing with enough angry husbands, a mental callus formed—a great asset, along with my crack wit and a sharp eye.

I shot him a quick smile. "Funny guy. Hell of a setup you have down here."

"Welcome to my home away from home." He raised his open palms, rotating to present the mechanical hideaway. "As you can see, I'm used to guests, unfortunately." He pointed to the cot we had ransacked earlier.

I rubbed my palms together, excited for any potential new information. And a new suspect. "What do you mean?" I asked, full well knowing the answer.

Clayton stared back as if I was joking. Playing dumb works out more often than you might think. It comes at the cost of looking like a dolt, but it pays the bills and disarms most. And it worked for Columbo. Fictional or not, he was one of the greats.

"Robert," Clayton said. "He owns the place, and he sure acts like it too. At first I'd find him snoring over there with the TV blasting. Figured it was safer having him here than doing who knows what somewhere else. I felt bad for the fool too, although all the gambling got him into this mess. And he's the boss, so who am I?"

I perked up. "You know him pretty well, I take it?"

"Ha. I used to. Was a pretty decent guy until the last year or so. He stopped coming by the mall for a while and just checked out. Then, a few weeks ago, he starts crashing here like I said. I let it slide until he started getting in the way, moving my stuff." The custodian looked around. "It's dangerous down here!"

Bart went into another coughing fit, this one more intense than the last. He regained his composure and excused himself, noting he didn't want to leave the upstairs unguarded. Good call—Robert was still out there somewhere and while Clayton could be the thief, it was smart thinking to split up.

I pivoted the conversation back on track as the young man scurried away. "Is that what the heated exchange was about? I couldn't help but notice the tension when I stopped by a few days ago."

"You saw that, huh?" He shook his head. "Yeah. Had enough of him sleeping down here, so I left him a note to clean up after himself. His mall sure, but I got a job to do. And it's just plain weird having him stalking around here late at night. Almost gave me a heart attack the other day. I told him to start acting like a boss and get himself together. He didn't like that. Taking it out on me ever since. I'll tell ya, I've worked here for years, and I've never been treated worse than I have in the last few weeks."

"What about the gambling you mentioned? What's that about?"

"Didn't outright tell me, but I found the betting slips. Not little bets. Big ones. Thousands. Makes sense why he wants to sell this place so badly. Unless he's been paying them off, he owes somebody big time. And from what I've seen around here lately, Robbie doesn't strike me as a guy that's ahead of the game, if you know what I mean." He pointed a chin at the bed of bottles.

"You see him around here recently?"

"Nope. And I've been scrubbing toilets across this place all night. I actually came down here to tuck him in," he laughed. "Naw. He wanted me to stop by on my way out. Told me he had another job for me." The janitor shrugged.

"It is pretty late. We figured you were gone since Forrest left. Bart said you usually carpool together?"

"Every now and then Robbie has me play gopher. Odds and ends, personal stuff usually. I told Forrest to not wait up and I'd catch an Uber or something." Clayton rolled his eyes. "And of course the dummy isn't here. Coulda saved a few bucks and left early."

I thanked Clayton for his time after getting a quick run-down of the intricate tunnel system. Just as Debbie described, the underground labyrinth reminded me of the hidden passages you'd find in a murder mystery. A killer, using the tunnels to sneak around undetected—unnoticed—until the timeline is pieced together and all is revealed. I took the janitor's advice and checked them out, bumbling through the warm, dark corridors until finding a set of stairs leading out. Surprisingly, this exit spilled out into a central part of the mall. As the door slammed behind, the brown edges blended perfectly with the wall, aside from the tiny, rusty keyhole. From Clayton's explanation, this was one of seven doors linked to the maze below. I laughed, imagining shoppers passing by hundreds of times without even realizing the secret world underneath—myself included.

Clayton was helpful and not what I had expected from the rough-looking man. But with a sack of money missing and only one other person wandering these halls, I couldn't ignore him as a suspect, even with Tiffany ruling him out. Could he have used the tunnels to creep by somehow, unnoticed?

A chill wafted by carrying the fresh scent of cinnamon rolls. With no bakers present, I suspected they were set to cook on a timer in the shop nearby. Either way, they smelled delicious and I was hungry. The quick walk towards the Cinnabon outlet was cut short.

"Boss!" Bart's voice shrieked from the walkie. "I found Mr. Robert. He's...he's dead!"

Chapter 15

I DARTED across the empty mall, almost slipping on the slick, freshly waxed flooring in not one, but three separate locations. Nestled between an abandoned department store and a cookware shop on its last legs, the emergency exit led outside to a red brick corridor lined with a few commercial size dumpsters. Walking into the cool air, I nearly tripped again over a heavy cement block propping the door open. The gum residue and cigarette butts scattered on the ground painted a picture of employees using the area for smoke breaks. Tonight, it was the final resting spot of one Robert Cunningham.

"I can't believe it," Bart said, his ghostly face tilted to the floor.

The young kid had clearly never seen a body before—and that wasn't a bad thing. It never gets any easier. And to be fair, other than at a few funerals, I've only found one on the job. Poor sucker cheating on his wife, keeled over mid... cheat. I figured my client wouldn't want pictures of a crime scene, so I stumbled in, confirmed the situation, and made my exit. Never got paid either, but I didn't have the heart to collect.

"Boss…" Bart leaned against a dumpster out of view from the body. "What…" he trailed off.

Hopes of cracking the case drifted away like Bart's empty eyes. My prime suspect, murdered. Was it the janitor after all? Or was my goofy dream girl behind this? My chance to figure it out had expired. I took another deep breath, exhaling my pride, and pulled out my phone.

"I'm calling the police." I punched the digits. "Call Tiffany. Just tell her it's urgent she come here."

"I—I… okay." The gaunt teen stumbled back into the building, shakily fumbling out his phone.

After making the call, I found Bart lingering near the doorway as if afraid of what was waiting outside. Not *as if*—I'm sure he was.

"You get a hold of her?" I asked.

"Yes sir, she's on her way. I called Miss Debbie too. I.. I left her a voicemail."

"Good. I hope you had enough coffee. This night is about to get even longer."

"I was worried you'd say that."

"Before you found him, did you see anything?"

"No sir. I stood around with Clayton for a few minutes while he waited for a ride. Then I started back on my patrol and…" He ran fingers over his face. "Poor Mrs. Tiffany. She's gonna be heart-broken when she gets here."

"Yeah? Seemed she had a curious relationship with her uncle, from what I saw."

"Sure." The young guard kicked a rock over in my direction. "They were at odds every now and again. But I know she cares about him. *Cared*. Wow, this is weird, man. Maybe I could go home?"

I studied his face, somber and drained of the Zagnut loving kid from earlier. "Look. It'll be okay, eventually. I promise. But right now, the police are going to have a lot of questions for us. I'll do my best to make them go easy on ya."

Bart snapped out of his trance and took a step back, hitting his shin against the doorframe. "Wait what? Why would they need to —you mean they might think *I* had something to do with this? My parents are gonna trip!"

Bart's reaction caused a realization of my own. I'd been so laser focused on Robbie as the thief. Now with the guy dead, a new set of questions rose. Of course Whodunnit. But was Robbie killed for stealing? I hated leaving a job unfinished, but what I heard next quashed the thought I'd be able to continue—sirens warbling in the distance.

Annoyance overshadowed any other emotion. I've dealt with the cops plenty, so I knew what came next. At least I've learned that references to the *Police Academy* movies rarely went over well. I braced myself for the next few hours. After they learn why I'm really here, well—my night was just beginning.

"Rise and shine."

I looked up to see the tall blonde woman slam the door shut. High cheekbones and pale eyes, probably Nordic descent. She carried herself with confidence, sauntering over before dropping the styrofoam cup with a plop. A dash of black gold flowed over the rim, landing on the table where my elbows once rested.

"I'm detective O'Connor," the late twenty-something said. She grabbed a chair and spun it to face me, straddling it backwards like one of the cool kids in *Saved by the Bell.*

I leaned back in my seat and glanced at my Casio—almost two in the morning. Over twenty minutes since they shuffled me into the real estate storefront, now doubling as an interrogation room.

"Ready for it to be over. To what do I owe the pleasure?" I said, then attacked the steaming java below.

A smirk and nod. "Only the best for Metro Detroit's World Class P.I."

"I haven't used those ads in years."

You make one stupid commercial and you never live it down.

"Kitschy, I liked the rip-off jingle you had at the end." She sucked in her lower lip and pulled a pen from the breast pocket of her button up. "What show was that?"

"*Perfect Strangers.*"

"No. No, that wasn't it. It was the one with the Urkel kid. Anyway, the sooner you get talking, the sooner you can leave. Unless you killed the guy, that is." She took a sip of her coffee, eyes burrowing a hole through my skull.

I fought the urge to tell her *Family Matters* was a spin-off of *Perfect Strangers.* "First day at work and I'm being fingered for murder? So much for job security. At least I'm on track to last longer than my time at K-Mart."

No reaction from the woman. "I hear you're in charge of security here. Why the change from your wannabe detective act?"

"Act? Dozens of satisfied Yelp reviews say otherwise!" I coughed and mumbled under my breath, "and the unsatisfied ones, too."

That garnered an eye roll from the investigator. Protecting my client's confidentiality was a top priority, but lying to the police wouldn't do me much good. And in a murder investigation, I wanted off the suspect list faster than the Tamagotchi craze lasted. I never could keep that little guy happy.

"I've always had a thing for malls, that's no secret." I chuckled and then sighed. "Have you talked to Tiffany yet?"

"I'll be direct with you, Paul. Some of us think you're a nuisance. Private eyes in general. But I remember my old partner saying you were alright. So yeah, we talked to her."

"No use beating around the bush then. Hopefully, she told you why I'm here. I was hired to catch someone stealing from the mall's coffers. The plan was to catch the thief in the act tonight. But instead, my number one suspect is being checked out by your field coroner out there."

I couldn't read the detective's expression, other than seeing she was deep in thought. Playing her cards close.

"You think he was the thief?" the detective asked.

I hesitated elaborating, but if I had any inclination to stay in the business, it helped having a cop on my side.

"All signs point to it," I started. "Motive. He wanted to sell the mall and his partners didn't. Make it look less profitable. And from the looks of it, he was down on his luck and needed the money... like yesterday. Access. He knew the schedules. The ins and outs of this place." I stopped to rake my forehead, fighting off a developing migraine. "And besides, the list of suspects is a bit bare."

"I heard you had an interesting night. Walk me through."

She must have gotten to my young sidekick first. I wonder what Bart had said? I started from the top, recalling the night. Complete with a list of the characters and a pretty solid timeline. The true detective listened intently, tapping the pen against her notepad when she wasn't scribbling.

After my account, she studied her writing. The pen made several hard loops around a single word before her eyes shot back to mine. "The sister. Deborah. When you walked her out, did you see her drive away?"

Did something happen to Debbie? My eyebrow raised like a certain wrestler-turned-actor-turned-wrestler. "Well, no. Wait.. why do you ask?"

The detective caught the flicker of apprehension in my voice. "Have something you want to share?"

"No. I just can't see her being involved with any of this."

"Well, I hate to burst your bubble. But the bag of cash we found in her locker says otherwise."

Chapter 16

"AND THEN SHE FIRED ME, just like that."

"Well, they found the money," Geri said, setting down a pint glass of her latest elixir—something bluish that smelled like raspberries. "You didn't expect to keep the job after they found the thief, did you?"

My neighbor had a point. But Tiffany seemed quick to cut me loose. Suspiciously quick. Or was I reading into things? Having full, all hours access to my favorite mall, then having it ripped away stung more than I imagined. My inner child took it personally.

"Yeah, I thought so," she said with a deep sigh, then plopped onto a couch across the room.

I crossed my arms. "You didn't have to cut your trip early on account of me."

"Is that so? It's after two in the afternoon. How long would you have slept if I hadn't come banging on your door?"

"Hey, I was up all night getting grilled by Detroit's Finest. Takes a lot outta ya."

"You seemed pretty out of it on the phone. And the radio silence thing afterwards had me worried. I already set up most of the hydroponic system, and I'll head back next week. That drive up north is beautiful this time of year. The trees..." The botanist stared off into the ether, as she often does. What was in that drink?

"Thank you. It's just… the case is closed, but it doesn't add up."

I shifted uncomfortably. "It doesn't make sense. Why would Debbie be stealing from the mall? And killing her uncle! What's her motive?"

"Are you sure you're not letting your rose-colored glasses get in the way, Sherlock?"

I thought back to the wacky woman dancing on the mall's CCTV screen. The goofball and her morning PA greetings. "Maybe, but it was clear she was content with owning her bookstore."

"I can't imagine the physical book business is doing so hot. Everything's digital these days. What if she needed the extra cash to keep afloat?"

I shot her a scowl. "Physical books make billions a year in the U.S. alone. And money didn't sound like a problem for her. She seemed like an outsider from the family. I got the sense that she was the only one that wanted the mall to survive. Arranging fun little events, her general attitude. Only my gut, but the girl actually cared about the place. Remember, you're not the only one that's good at reading people. I've been catching cheaters and liars for years. I didn't get anything like that from her. Her family, on the other hand..."

"So what are you going to do now? You're off the case, as they say. Right?"

"Nothing says I can't do a little shopping." I flashed her a wink.

Just as suspected, a rusty metal security gate blocked the entrance to Sleuths. The smell of magic marker still lingered on the plain white paper taped to the glass behind the bars. '*Closed Until Further Notice*'.

"Hey, I thought I heard you got canned." The voice took me by surprise.

I turned to see Hakim, the newly engaged employee of the closed bookstore.

"And I thought you were on vacation." My tone was dry, fully hardboiled, if that's a thing.

His eyes flashed a single, involuntary blink. "This year's HorrorCon can wait. Not everyday your boss is charged with multiple felonies, including murder. Plus, she's innocent, I might add."

"What makes you say that?"

Eyes widened while his head slumped in disbelief. "Because she is. C'mon! You've met her. You can't think what they're saying is true! Killer and a thief? Give me a break. She's the nicest boss I've ever had. Too nice if you ask me."

"You seem confident. Why so?"

"Well, she's a total geek, for one. We aren't usually the killing type. And Mr. Cunningham may have been older, but he's a strong dude. Unless Deb's hiding some super healing powers, she couldn't have physically done it. Girl finally ditched the shoulder sling, but she's still in physical therapy from the accident a few months back. She can barely lift a fifteen pound box of books! How could she have landed any kinda killing blow?" He paused to look around and lowered his voice to a conversational volume. "And more importantly, last year, when the Sleuths was raking in the dough from some big author signings, she was paying double the rent to help keep the mall afloat. *Voluntarily*. That sound like a thief?"

It didn't. But the police didn't seem to agree, especially with all the evidence. Could she have been playing me and everyone else? There weren't many other leads and I've been fooled before. I shifted my posture, channeling more of that private eye wit.

"So," I said. "If she didn't do it, who did?"

Hakim grew uneasy, as if a chill washed over his body. "Hell, I don't know. I can't picture anyone here doing it, eccentric as they are."

"Her sister?"

"Tiffany? She is just as annoying as her husband. They're a pain, but I can't see them killing anyone. Or stealing from their own mall."

"What is Tiffany's husband's deal?

"Wyatt? He drops in and tries to order us around like he owns the place, even though he's got no official say. He's an ass, but I see through his wall street act. You know the type? Ruthless on the outside, nervous insecure jerk on the inside."

"You sure he doesn't have a little Patrick Bateman in him?"

"Who?"

"Nevermind," I said. Even if he didn't watch movies, I figured he'd catch the *American Psycho* reference. It started off as a book, *after all.* "So if it's no one from the mall, are you saying it was random?"

"You're the security guy. Or you were." The young man smirked. "Deb didn't talk to her uncle much, but I knew she was worried about the guy. Seemed like he had money problems. I guess now that I think about it, he probably got caught up in a loan gone bad. Hate to say it, but he was kind of an ass."

Some of Hakim's theory made sense. But it had holes. The money in Deb's locker had to be related. And I wouldn't be the best private eye in town if I didn't follow every lead. Or second best, according to my biggest competition in town, Alan Langstreet.

"I was here all night," I said. "You saying someone from outside snuck in, clobbered the guy and dumped his body? Possible, but it sounds like a long shot. Got any other theories?"

Being a top sleuth didn't mean I had to figure it all out myself. Work smart, not hard, right?

"You really think someone from here did it?" Hakim asked. "Like you said, you were here that night. Start with who was here, I guess. Good luck figuring it out." Slicker than a magician, Hakim shot a business card from his sleeve and flicked it out between his fingers. "I mean it. Deb's a good one. If I can help in any way, call."

I was half expecting the business card to disappear in my hand—the smooth, expensive paper confirming I correctly guessed the man's second job, revealed in beautiful glossy gold letters. And with that, the part-time bookseller, part-time magician sauntered away, his hand grazing the railing overlooking the mall courtyard. He was right about one thing—I had a good idea of who was here and where I would go next.

The walk to Hot Topic was uneventful but surprisingly crowded. Apparently, a body at the local mall is one way to increase foot traffic. Not a sustainable one, though. The store looked just like I remembered it back in my twenties: dark, small, and filled with all sorts of pop culture shirts and toys from yesterday and today.

"Some things never change," I chuckled under my breath while thumbing through a t-shirt rack with bands older than most of the shoppers.

"Can I help you?" an annoyed clerk scoffed.

I hid a laugh at the coincidence—the young employee wearing a Depeche Mode shirt. "You got any magic eye posters back there?" I received a confused shrug and pressed on. "Say, is Julie in today? She was holding something for me."

The manager, Randy according to the nametag, squinted for far too long. Either the platinum blond hair was bothering his eyes, or something was up.

"You're that security guy, aren't you? She's not here. No call, no showed today."

How... *ponderous, man.* "That typical of her?" I asked.

"Julie?" He guffawed loudly and regained his composure after looking around the store to see it went unnoticed. "We don't call her Lisa Simpson for nothing. That girl is the biggest rule follower I've ever known. Makes the rest of my team look bad." He pointed to another employee, and as if on cue, the blue-haired boy dropped a box of toy capsules sending them bouncing. Randy shook his head like it was a common occurrence. "Not very difficult around here, as you can see."

"I hope she's all right. She was worried about hearing from her dad when I saw her."

Another squint from the manager. "Hey, word is you were fired after they found that body. I think you should leave." And like that, the room grew cold and Randy's lips pursed tight.

I was on to something, but I didn't know just what.

"HEY BOSS," a nervous sounding voice greeted me outside the store. "I mean, uh, what do I call you now?

"Hey Bart. Paul's fine."

"That's hmm... okay. Paul. Hi Paul. Uhm. I hate asking you but, well... I was told to ask you to leave."

"I was just leaving, thanks." Wow, Randy sure had security on speed dial.

Bart looked around and turned beet red.

"What is it Bart?"

"I didn't mean the store. The mall. I'm supposed to make sure you leave and escort you out."

That makes a bit more sense. *Or does it?*

"Let me guess." I shook my head. "Tiffany, right?"

"Actually, it was her husband. He was watching you on the cameras and said it's a bad look having you here right now with the... you know, the police stuff. I'm really sorry."

My former apprentice reluctantly motioned to exit, his palm trembling.

"It's okay Bart, I'm leaving. Hey, I'll even let you walk me the whole way out."

During the trip through the sugary smelling air, I reflected on all the walks I've had in this place. Excited, youthful walks toward the arcade as a teen. Slow Christmas shopping walks, bumping into what seemed like the entire city buying last-minute gifts for loved ones. Empty, sad walks, watching store after store go from clearance sale to emptiness. And only recently, the behind the scenes walk, free to explore wherever I please—in sunlight, moonlight—all in total silence. Today though, a walk of shame. Being escorted by a nervous kid who appeared to be struggling with his emotions. I tried to make it easier on him, he was following orders after all.

"So uh, this is it, boss. I mean Paul." The young guard leaned into the heavy glass door to the parking lot. "Really sorry again."

"Say Bart, can I ask you something? Outside?" The audio on the security system was atrocious, but outside, it was non-existent. The former coworker followed, stopping to lean against the brick wall with an even more confused expression.

A cool blast of wind hit the security officer's face. From the shivers and arm rubbing, I figured I didn't have much time with him—despite the warm sun beating down, the short sleeve uniform was way underdressed for the chill.

"Bart, what's going on here? Why's Tiffany's husband calling the shots?"

He looked around apprehensively, eyes trailing a pickup truck driving much too fast for a parking lot. "Mrs. Tiffany said with everything going on, her husband is going to be helping out. To consider him in charge."

Was that fear on his face? I wondered if Bart saw a different version of Wyatt than Hakim. "How often does he get involved in mall business?" I asked.

Bart winced. "I'm really not supposed to be talking to you." A loud sigh. "But I don't think Miss Debbie did it. I swear I saw her drive off. And we took turns watching that hallway all night. It just doesn't make sense."

Bart's eyes darted to the glass entry doors while he took a step closer. I was almost outatime.

"Bart, remember that girl that stopped by after hours?"

"Julie?"

"Yeah, what do you know about her?"

"Julie Carpenter. I've seen her around a bunch. I don't know much about her. She's been working here for the last year or so. Took a gap year before college that turned into three. She's dating Billy." His face turned to a grimace. "I think they live together."

If that's not knowing much, Bart's brain must be overflowing.

"Why the face?" I asked.

"Billy was a security guard on the morning shifts for a while here, before he took a new job. I just miss him is all. We kind of lost touch, never returns my calls. He was a little weird. Reminds me of you."

"Thanks." We all need a friend like Bart, tells it like it is. "Do you know where they live? I'd like to stop by and see how she's doing." *And maybe ask a question or two.*

"I think they're in Troy, off the—"

"Bart." A heavy door slammed intentionally from behind. "You can head back in. They need you at the record store."

Just when it was getting good. Bart scurried back into the mall, leaving me with the man I instantly knew was Wyatt Price, Tiffany's husband. White, fifty or so, box dyed short jet black hair. A well-tailored suit wrapped his obviously athletic frame. First impressions were often important, and if we're playing word association here, the only thing that came to mind was the word weasel.

"I've heard a lot about you, Mr. Washington." The tall man said, all business in his tone. "I truly apologize for having you sent away. It's all about optics, I'm afraid. As you know, the mall hasn't been doing so well and we'd rather not inflame an already sensitive topic."

I'm sure, buddy. Wyatt's facial expressions seemed rehearsed. If Uncle Robbie was an 80s movie villain, this guy was the 90s equivalent. I hid the smile, pushing down the daydreams of Jackie Chan giving him a blast of drunken fist punches.

"Business is business, I get it. Where's the missus?" I asked.

"Grieving, naturally. She's had ups and downs with her uncle, but family is family."

"Like her sister."

"Unfortunate. We had our suspicions, of course." He gestured an open palm in my direction. "I'm certain you would have figured her out, had she not escalated her crimes. A shame really."

Wyatt's eyes drifted over my shoulder. A twitch of anger danced over his lips. I turned to see a news van drive past the old steakhouse sharing a parking lot with the mall.

"Optics." He let the word linger before continuing. "I had planned to contact you personally, but as you can understand, we've been quite busy with everything right now. We appreciate everything you've done for us." A hand dove into the suit coat, returning with a beige slip of paper that would soon have me questioning my ethics. The check swayed in the breeze, held between his index and middle fingers. "For your troubles and time."

I grit my teeth. A guy's gotta eat. I grabbed the check and tucked it in my pocket without glancing at the amount.

"Thank you for your services, Mr. Washington," he added. "I hope you understand this officially terminates your contract and involvement in our affairs."

I nodded and shook the waiting hand. The saunter to my car was slow and deliberate. This wasn't the first time someone had tried to pay me off, but it *was* the first time I took the offer. *The check isn't cashed yet*, I thought.

Keys in the ignition, I turned my rearview mirror to catch Channel 7's bubbly blonde on-site reporter march onto the scene, strutting into my childhood mall to report on a murder.

With a deep exhale, I pulled out the check and studied all the zeros. The last payday this big was from a TV reunion movie over a decade ago. Another deep sigh and I started the engine, listening to the DeLorean purr until I heard the smooth silky sounds of

Crockett's Theme—the slow, melodic music that would play when Don Johnson graced the TV set on *Miami Vice*. The trouble with having such a jam as your ringtone is having to answer the call.

"Washington P.I. speaking," I said to the unknown number.

"Paul. This is Detective O'Connor. We need to talk."

Chapter 18

A KNOCK on the driver's side window yanked me from the dreamy vaporwave beats blasting through the car speakers.

"Woah!" I said while unrolling the window manually. "You got here fast."

"I was in the neighborhood," the stoic cop said. "Nice ride, Marty. From what I've heard about you, I shouldn't be surprised."

O'Connor sauntered to the passenger side, pulled the door open, and then collapsed onto the well-maintained, albeit cracked, leather.

"Make yourself at home," I said with a chortle. "Am I in trouble?"

"Oh, if you were, you'd know." Her eyes briefly floated from the steaming mug in her gloved hands to me. "Trust me."

"I take it this isn't a personal call."

"You wish, Washington." She chuckled.

We settled in, both staring at the sprawling aged shopping complex in the distance.

The cop cleared her throat. "Something isn't adding up here. I hate to say it, but I need your help. I'm not getting anywhere."

A tinge of relief—not that I was too worried. But after being found at the scene of a murder, the sudden visit was off putting. Especially with how our last meeting ended.

"What can I do ya for, officer?" I immediately regretted the stupid response.

She ignored it. "My number one suspect is locked up and can't make bail. All signs point to her. Case closed. *On paper.*" She let the last words linger.

"She didn't do it."

"That's what I'm afraid of."

"You, afraid?" I smiled, although she didn't catch it. The conversation lacked eye contact, both of us still locked on the mall.

"You're still technically a person of interest." It was more of a warning than a threat. "But like I said before, my partner trusted you. Don't prove him wrong."

Sometimes, it's all about who you know. My dad was a cop. We were pretty close too, having as much of a normal life as possible for his odd hours. Until the divorce. After my folks split, mom zipped my nine year old self off to Hollywood, and the rest is history. It only lasted a few years, with Mom and I having enough of the chaos out West, bringing us back to good ole Michigan. I reconnected with dad afterwards, trying to resume a regular teenage life despite being a semi-famous child star at the time. Dad must have talked me up before he retired from the force.

I snapped out of the daydream. "What do you need from me?" I asked.

"You were on the inside. What's your theory?"

I shifted in my seat. An opportunity to clear my crush's name, falling on my lap like this? What are the chances?

"You've got the wrong guy. Girl. Whatever. Midwest thing, we're all guys."

"So you've said. Why?" she asked, slightly adjusting in the leather to face my direction.

"First of all—motive. There isn't any. At least for the theft. Why would Debbie steal from the mall? She's been trying to save the place. In fact, it seems like between her sister and uncle, she was the only one taking initiative. The bookstore looked quite profitable, from what I gathered. Not to mention she didn't have access to the safe."

"Are you sure about that?"

"Yeah, remember what I told you? I saw her standing around that night, waiting for Tiffany."

O'Connor nodded. "What I'm about to tell you stays here. And if you talk, I'll know."

I pantomimed zipping my lips.

"In addition to the bag of money we found in Deborah's locker, her prints were all over a pipe that forensics believes was the murder weapon. I'm still waiting to confirm what went down, but the D.A. thought it was more than enough to hold her."

"I'm telling you, you got the wrong woman."

"That's why I'm here. She doesn't fit the bill. I'm going off my gut right now, but it's got me to where I am today. Something is wrong here." She took a big sip of coffee before continuing. "Take me back to that night. Was there anything you didn't tell me? Anything you left out?"

I thought back to the interrogation. Somewhat in shock, I was mostly exhausted from the all-nighter. "Pretty sure we covered it all. Me and Bart patrolled the place, taking turns watching that office, the whole night. Until I realized the cameras weren't recording. Went to look in the safe, empty. Patrolled around and eventually Bart found the body. Not much to it."

"Can you tell me any more about the security system?"

"The cameras? Like I already said, they weren't recording. I can't give you much more since I wasn't focused on that room. It could have been from the power surge after that girl stopped by."

"I remember you mentioned her. Julie..." The detective's voice trailed off.

"That doesn't sound good."

"Yeah. We can't find her. Boyfriend is worried. Says she's not one to up and leave like that."

"She was really concerned when I saw her. But I figured it was just a kid worried about her missing phone. She said something about her dad being out of the country. I'm getting some suspicions that wasn't entirely true."

I filled her in on the awkward exchange with Julie's manager, incorporating at least three references to the store's Hello Kitty merch.

"Ok. I get it. Anything else?" she asked.

My mind flooded with visions of empty, sprawling liminal spaces. Long stretches of shadowy hallways blanketed in moonlight. The cracks and creaks of old steel and wood swaying in the quiet night. Even darker tunnels connecting boiler rooms, abandoned offices, and masses of piping and metal. The thought seemed important, but not enough to verbalize coherently.

"No. But thanks for reaching out. I know she's innocent, and I'm not going to let her take the fall for someone else."

We turned to each other for the first time in minutes.

A smile crossed her lips. "At the risk of sounding like one of your favorite TV cops, don't get in our way. But off the record, let me know what you come up with."

Chapter 19

"SERIOUSLY, SHE SAID *OFF THE RECORD*?" Corey pushed his neck out, making his already big head protrude. "And she said to keep all this a secret? You know, everything you just told me?"

He looked around to find the pawnshop empty. Of people, that is. The musty medium-sized space was filled wall to wall with knick knacks and electronics, a majority from my favorite periods, the eighties and nineties.

"How long have I known you?" I scanned a glass cabinet filled with movie themed trading cards before settling back on the long-haired shop owner. "Two decades? If I can't trust you not to blab, we've got a problem."

"Safe with me. I love a good mystery. So what's next for my fancy pants detective friend?

"*Officially*, I'm off the case."

"Going rogue, *Maverick*?" the shopkeeper said with a sly grin.

"You know it. Thanks to my new police friend, I'm on my way to check on a lead. Or a loose end."

"Ah right. You want that package I called you about?" Corey knelt under a glass case with enough gold trinkets and coins to make a leprechaun jealous. He returned holding a tiny brown cardboard box, the shape of a paperback. "I get you love checking out the laserdiscs, and of course seeing your old pal, but you really need to update your address. Space is money in this business."

I took the box and studied the label with caution, immediately recognizing the handwriting. I tried to hide my reaction. "I love seeing ya Corey, but I changed my address over a month ago."

A big sigh from the jolly, slightly older man. "I had a feeling. I'm getting less junk, but it's still coming." He tugged at his bushy red beard. "You think it's *another one?"*

"I don't know anyone from Hollywood Hills..." My nose scrunched up like I smelled something rank. *Another one.* Last month, the pawnshop received a postcard addressed to me—not uncommon—I was using the store to collect letters and residual checks while I procrastinated on updating my info with the post office. But this mail was different. And not in a good way. A cryptic message or a sick joke from an anonymous sender, addressed from San Diego. Either way, I couldn't get it out of my head for weeks. Corey thought I was crazy—reading too much into it. I stared at the package, frozen, hoping he was right and that this was just another Jelly of Month I forgot to cancel.

"Well, you gonna open it?" the redheaded pawn owner said, rubbing his hands together.

"Aren't you worried it could take out the store?"

Corey's face changed from eagerness to fear. "On second thought, just let me know what's in there later, okay? I'm sure it's nothing, like I've been telling you."

Did I really think it would explode? No. But I wanted some privacy—despite being friends forever, Corey didn't need to know everything. And that first postcard felt personal: *"I wish you would have said something"* in a strangely familiar, beautiful cursive script. On the back, a nighttime shot of Pismo Beach. The message didn't ring any bells, but I took it as a threat—*I Know What You Did Last Summer* style. If there truly was a secret I was lugging around, it was deep and buried. And if I've learned anything from horror movies, some secrets are best left underground.

"Will do, Iceman," I said, channeling my most confident facial expression and pushing away thoughts of a stalker. Or secret admirer? "I gotta get going. Text me if someone drops off a Dreamcast, I haven't been able to fix the disc drive on mine."

The owner nodded, then spun on a barstool, resuming the game of Turtles II he left paused on the CRT behind. Back at the car, I gave the box one more look before stowing it in the trunk, hoping I'd forget about it until the next deep detailing a year from now.

Julie's house was only a few miles away from the pawnshop. The ten-minute drive forced my brain to shift gears back to the case at hand.

A small, thousand square foot red-brick ranch on the outskirts of Detroit, Julie and her boyfriend had made a cute little home for themselves. From the outside, I wouldn't have guessed a pair of young, early twenty-somethings would be sporting all the lawn gnomes and looking glass orbs. In fact, the tulip-filled lawn reminded me of my grandma's old house, located smack dab in the middle of Hamtramck, even closer to Detroit.

I parked my car against the curb, a few houses down the sleepy suburban street. After buying it, I quickly learned that a DeLorean wasn't the best for a private eye. It garnered lots of attention and didn't help with being discreet. In fact, that was the reason for my second car, an old Dodge coupe that fit in with every setting—except time travel.

The slow saunter across the bumpy sidewalk had me second guess my choice of vehicles today, passing not one, but two elderly men watering their grass, one with a cigarette hanging on for its dear life.

"Hey. Nice car. You some kinda movie star?" the man said with a thick European accent.

The gruff voice sounded like a late night horror host from the Detroit area—although this wasn't a Wolfman by any stretch. From his facial features, I imagined him one of the many Polish immigrants that moved to the area in the sixties.

"Something like that," I said. Context told me he was focused on the car, and not a fan of my childhood acting. "Nice day for this time of year."

"Sure is," he said, the cigarette bobbing on his lip while he spoke. "Haven't seen you around here."

If there's one thing I've learned from the detective gig—and there's been a few things—it's that you can crack a case at any moment, from the least likely of places. While I had doubts this bald septuagenarian in a bathrobe was going to blast my case wide open, he was the neighbor of my next lead.

"I'm just headed over to Julie's." I pointed to the house next door, laughing at the silly piratey cartoon skull and crossbones flag above the mailbox. "You know 'em?"

The man tapped to ash before a final puff, then flicked the butt into the street. "Yeah, little bit. Interesting couple. You a friend of theirs or something?"

"Or something," I smiled. "They around?"

"Haven't seen the girl in a few days, not that I'm lookin'." The neighbor fished out a fresh pack of smokes and popped a new one in his mouth while talking. "Billy usually works late. Don't see his car, so he's not home either. Comes back after midnight usually. I can see the damn lights of his work car beam into my windows. Stupid woodpecker security logo. Pisses me off just thinking about it. "

"Thanks for the info. They called me over," I lied. "Maybe someone borrowed their car."

The man shrugged and resumed the watering, leaving a huge pool of water glittering at the edge of his lawn.

As expected, the rapping on the door and ding dongs went unanswered. Before heading down the blue wood planks of the porch, I snuck a peek into the mailbox next to the door, overflowing with a few days worth of letters. Not a good sign.

On the way to my car, the avid smoker and water enthusiast stopped me again. "Told ya they aren't home," he said with an ear to ear grin.

"If either of them come by, give me a call." Remembering how cool Hakim's trick was, I channeled a bit of my own magic. Using the sleight of hand I picked up in my younger years on set with a Vegas magician, I flicked a glossy business card from thin air, presenting it to the smoker.

Almost dropping the cigarette out of his mouth, he grabbed the card and scanned it before his eyes returned to mine. "Detective, huh? They in trouble?"

"Let's hope not," I said.

Chapter 20

THAT "WOODPECKER" logo turned out to be no woodpecker at all. Robust Robin was one of Detroit's biggest security contractors, and coincidentally my biggest competitor. When I first started P.I. work in the city, I was lucky to get any work, thanks to their gigantic advertising budget.

I made a quick search on my phone to confirm their new headquarters opened just a few miles off the freeway. After grabbing a bite at the local coney, I cruised toward Eastern Market to see if I could get any intel on Julie's boyfriend. A flimsy lead, but it was all I had. And my schedule was free—in a twist of irony, I had referred all my calls to the competitor to take the big mall job.

Being a Saturday with decent sunny weather, the market part of Eastern Market was bustling. Rows of flower vendors lined the street selling beautiful buds from crimson to cyan, every in-season greenery you could imagine. Mouth-watering BBQ scents wafted through my open window, a combination of smells from the multiple roadside grills. A few local restaurants joined in, pop-ups set up by the block party cookout in the alleyways. I hadn't visited the area in a while, so it was nice to see it hopping and bumpin'. Warbled bass thumped from speakers in the distance—the unmistakable piano of a nineties house track drifting over the ambient sounds of shoppers.

The seller's area was just as busy: a giant, modernized barn was packed with vendors; across the way, a street of butcher shops and antique stores. What the market's name didn't describe, however, was the sprawling warehouses surrounding the vibrant hub. Only a block or two away, countless aging brick and concrete relics of industry left their scars, many abandoned for decades. Past the empty, overgrown fields, and nestled in between one of these artifacts, stood the newly renovated two story office of Robust Robin. Despite the rumors they were involved in some shady business practices, I had to give them credit for helping the city. Their small plot of land stood out from aging, empty rows of decay and broken-windowed factories. From the gorgeous flowery landscaping and red brick sidewalk, to the brand new brushed nickel street lights, the space invited new businesses to an often overlooked area.

I parked in the impressively secure-looking gated lot when the song "Dear Mama" played through my car speakers.

"Hi Mom," I said to the windshield. I never knew where they hid the microphone in the after-market setup.

"Hi sweetie. Was that you?" My mom was the best, but details were not her strong suit.

"Depends," I laughed. "Where might you be?"

"Flower shopping with your dad. I saw your car. It had to be you!"

Like I've said before, this car is not discrete. Only one of a dozen in the Metro area, if the message boards are to be believed. And I took pride in keeping it in tip-top shape.

"You were driving too fast!" she continued. "There's so many people around. You are lucky your dad was busy looking for peppers."

Did I mention my parents remarried? As if a pair of fated mates in one of her favorite romance novels, after I hung up my Hollywood hat and we returned to Detroit, they reconnected during a surprise Christmas visit. They weren't expecting to see each other that night, but the awkward, romcom-esque dinner led to them talking again. And the rest is history, including him retiring soon after. Even though he loved the job, he regretted not joining us for my acting career and they picked up like it never happened.

"How's dad doing these days?" I asked.

"Oh, you know him. Always keeping busy. He worries about you. I have to talk him out of calling you at least once a week. He's always saying you should leave things to the police."

Dad wasn't keen on my new career from the get-go. I was still shocked that he likely put in a good word with O'Connor's partner.

"Don't worry mom, I can take care of myself," I mumbled, reverting into a defiant teen.

"Good. Did you see what happened at Lakeview? Such a shame. I remember taking you there all the time when you were a baby. You loved those cheese pretzels. Hot Stans?"

"Sad stuff, yeah," I said flatly, not correcting her on Hot Sam's or the mall. Before changing its name decades ago, Lakeview Mall was one of the only shopping centers in town. The *Are You Afraid of the Dark* style rumor on the playground told the story of a body floating in the surrounding lake. Soon after, they changed the name to Mayview, filled and paved over the lake, and never spoke about it again. Back in my twenties, I searched around for any reference to the story and came up empty—Yahoo and AskJeeves only took me so far. Now almost fifty years later, only a rare few even remembered the original name—my mom being one.

"Honey, we have to go," she said. "Call us sometime, okay? The Penhallows are stopping by next week. You should come by. Their daughter just got divorced too."

"You got it, mom." Hopefully she didn't hold me to it.

"And dad says to slow down or you'll get a ticket. I guess he saw you."

The call ended, and as always, the cute surprise brought a silly smile to my face. Until I turned back to the dark brick building and caught an overly curious uniformed man approaching.

"This is a private area, sir," the young, well-built young Asian man said, hunched over a few feet from the open window. "I don't believe we're expecting any visitors today."

"I'm Dirk Daring, surprise inspection."

Clearly not a fan of the old arcade game *Dragon's Lair,* the uniform had no reaction. Instead, he stood tall. Very tall. With a finger to his ear, the man studied my face, then nodded, whispering "Yes sir" to what I realized was an earpiece.

"I apologize, Mr. Washington," the dark-haired man said, extending his arm, palm open toward the office. "Please, be our guest."

Alan must have kept tabs on me, I thought to myself. A few months ago, I was offered a position with the outfit. Or was it a buyout? Either way, it would have been decent money with flexible hours. And questionable clients. The pros were nice, but I enjoyed being my own boss way too much. Other than working for my clients. Much to his dismay, I declined.

Following the lumbering specimen of fitness into RR HQ, I prepared to see a row of similarly dressed universal soldiers waiting to greet us. Instead, we entered the sleek office, wall to wall matte white paint surrounding the lone secretary at their desk. A trickling LED fountain flowed in the center of the lobby, translucent beads of dark indigo water dripping from the second story to the pool below. Enough plants to make Geri jealous flanked the walls—some potted, some hanging, and even some growing on the windows. A large neon robin flickered above the floating steps to the second floor, its red glow both comforting and fear-inducing. There was something sinister about the smile on the bird's face.

"Paul!" Someone shouted from above. I saw it was Alan, pressed against the railing of the second story, motioning to join.

The second floor was one large open glass boardroom. A fish-bowl, some would say. Compared to the room, the deep brown walnut table was rather small, only fitting eight expensive leather chairs. It reminded me of the OCP boardroom from a certain movie about Detroit's first cyborg cop. Except we weren't in a highrise. And unless I missed it, no giant robot mechs.

Alan dismissed a gaggle of uniformed men and waved me through the streak-free doors, then turned to my host. "Thanks Lawrence. I'll call you if I need you."

Here I was again, face to face with Alan Langstreet. A few years younger and a few pounds heavier, the man ranked high among Detroit's most successful young black entrepreneurs. And by heavier, I mean muscle. He put Lawrence to shame, almost busting out of the size too small button up. I envied his sense of style. Pink, green, and blue shapes adorned his black necktie. Suspenders continued the aesthetic, connecting to a dark pair of Brooks Brothers slacks. Judging by appearances alone, this guy had everything I'd want in a best friend.

"You never returned my calls," he said, confidence radiating from his gaze. "I can't say I'm surprised. A man of your talents turning down…" He opened his hands to the impressive skylight. "All of this," he laughed.

I couldn't tell if that was a compliment or an insult.

"I can't tell if that was a compliment or an insult," I decided to ask.

"Oh, come now." He waved me to the table and took a seat. "Sit. Want something to drink?" He didn't give me a chance to answer and tapped at his ear. "Suze, two Dark 'N' Stormies, please. Hold the dark." These guys and their earpieces. Bart and I did just fine with walkies. "I take it by that look of disgust that you're not here to accept my offer, are you?"

I had a bad habit of not hiding my jealousy. "What you're seeing is awe. Nice place you have here, Al. Can I call you Al?"

"I'd rather you not. And thank you. It's been a lot of hard work, as I'm sure you know."

"Oh, I'm *sure*," I said, putting a little extra mustard on that hotdog. "You have quite the reputation."

Alan propped his elbows on the table with clasped hands. After a few seconds of silence, he cracked his knuckles and leaned back in the leather. "Then what do I owe the honor of this visit?"

I followed his lead and settled in the chair. *Man alive, was it comfortable.* Better than the unforgiving wooden torture device in my office. "I'm looking for someone."

"Aren't we all," Alan snickered. "I guess you're not as good a detective as I thought."

"Hilarious." I paused while his assistant carried in a silver tray with two twenty ounce bottles of Faygo Ginger Ale. Dark and stormy alright. "Billy. He works nights for you. Used to work at Mayview until recently."

"Mayview Mall." Alan's dark complexion grew rosier while he shifted in his seat. *Curious.* "Such a tragedy." His tone lacked any shred of empathy.

"Yeah, it was a bummer. Guy got a real *Killer Deal at Mayview Mall.*" I winked at you, dear reader, like Ferris Bueller breaking the fourth wall.

"Rumors say you were working it when things went down."

"The only rumors I listen to are by Fleetwood Mac."

"You have quite the rep too, *smart guy.*" Alan twisted the cap off his bottle. After taking in the satisfying fizz, he poured the amber soda into a crystal glass. "Help yourself." He nudged the tray of drinks.

"I'm more of a Vernor's guy myself. So about Billy."

"Is he in trouble?"

I shook my head. "His girlfriend."

"Hm. Billy is working across town at Sunset Mall. When we lost the contract at Mayview, I shifted a few of my men over there. Billy was too good to let go."

"You had Mayview?" I played dumb.

Alan hesitated before answering. "I did. A small one. Until the owner downsized to her own ragtag crew." I swear he shot me a look. "I even offered a discount on armored car transports, but she declined. I guess things are as bad as they look."

His high-pitched laugh was annoying. And there wasn't anything funny here except his story countered Tiffany's. Just how bad were things at Mayview?

"You run into any crime there? Any thefts?" I asked.

After a big swig from the glass, he set it down hard. "I still want you to join my team, so I'll play ball. No, nada. Easiest contract in the world. Shame the place will probably get split up and sold, although maybe that's a good thing. More businesses to protect. Now if you'll excuse me." He stood, pushing his chair out aggressively. "I have a meeting in five minutes. If you change your mind, you know where to reach me."

I smoothed out the No Doubt sticker on my dash, then started the engine. Alan seemed like a straight shooter, although a tad suspicious. If he truly wasn't aware of any thefts, there was a high likelihood none happened. Why would Tiffany lie? Without a thief, what was I even hired for in the first place? Her story stunk, and I was out of those tiny scented tree things. I needed to have a chat with my former boss, but first, a little trip to visit Billy at Sunset Mall.

Chapter 21

A HALF HOUR down the freeway stood Sunset Mall. Split into two giant sections, the mall was connected by a beautiful glass-window skywalk. Hovering above the oddly named Big Beaver road, cars zipped underneath as the moving sidewalk propelled me closer to what locals dubbed "the rich side". Both sections of the mall were elegant, filled with fine dining, shopping, and everything in between. But the ritzier side housed the stores able to afford their massive rent on the sale of a single designer t-shirt.

Although it was less than a quick drive away, the scene at Sunset was a stark comparison to the bleak, empty, aging walls of Mayview. Crowds of teens and older folk strutted around carrying bags of expensive wares and held overpriced coffees. Walking with a purpose, they glided over the marble tiled flooring from one luxury shop to the next. Luxury indeed—the mall even had fancy cloth-like paper towels in the crystal clean restrooms.

Entering from the slightly more reasonable three story side, a quick glance at the mall directory showed my destination was across the way. This place wasn't my usual stomping ground. Even after running into some money from the acting gig, I'd always preferred the other malls in town—Mayview and Oakmill. Sunset was clean, big, and had some cool stores, sure. But it was *too* bright, *too* polished for my nineties loving self. And it didn't have an arcade. Moot point now, with Sunset being the sole survivor of the mall wars. Or at least things appeared to be heading that way.

A speaker above the travelator buzzed, "Escalator ends. Please watch your step."

I hopped off the moving track with a youthful zest, garnering scoffs from a family dressed in furs. *A nice reminder of why I didn't come here often.*

Past the giant lobby's grand piano, a set of stairs led down into the security area. While some malls like Mayview spared every expense for areas the public wouldn't see, this mall had another approach. In fact, the employee corridor was just as ornate as the rest of the place. Black and cream marbled floors, rich viridian green walls, and flickering, candle-like sconces illuminated the way to a thick tinted door labeled Security.

Before my knuckle could land, the door swung open, revealing a tall, rather thin white guy in his early twenties. The blue Sunset Mall baseball cap matched his uniform, wrinkled with a few noticeable stains I wouldn't expect from the glitzy place.

"You must be Paul," the young man said, running fingers over a ten o'clock shadow. "I'm Billy. They radioed over to expect you. Have you found her?"

When I arrived at Sunset, I mistook an overly helpful mall cop for Julie's boo. Mentioning Billy's missing girlfriend earned me a straight shot to the man himself.

"No, but that's why I'm here," I said, crossing my arms.

His solemn expression warped into defeat. "Then *why* are you here? You a cop?"

"No again, but I'm working with them." It wasn't a lie, exactly.

"I've already told them everything. It's hard enough getting through a shift." He took a step back and leaned against the closed door. "And my lawyer says I shouldn't talk to anyone."

"I saw her that night, Billy. I may be the last person to have seen her."

The young officer's pupils dilated, sweeping the cramped, dark hallway. After another sigh, he cocked his head toward the lapel on his collar. "347 here. I'm taking my fifteen minutes now."

More high tech. What ever happened to good ole fashioned walkie talkies?

I didn't want to love it for the price tag alone. But man, this coffee was tasty. Smooth, with just the right amount of bitter. And the smell was unbelievable. This was easily the best cup of iced coffee since craft services on the set of my old show.

"Okay," Billy said while massaging his neck. "The cops didn't tell me anything about this. Are you sure she said it was her dad?"

"Damn sure." I leaned back in the hard teak chair. So the fancy coffee shop got something wrong, the seating was uncomfortable as all hell. They probably didn't want people to linger.

Billy shook his head, then propped his elbows on the reclaimed wood planks. "Her dad up and left two years ago. I think the jerk is somewhere in Europe. Wrote this really nasty letter to Julie and her brother. We've been living at her grandma's place now after she moved to a nursing home. Tried taking care of Grams, but it was a lot with me and Jules always working."

"You think she was hiding something from you?"

Billy's eyes narrowed. A flicker of... *anger*?

"I take that as a yes," I said.

"I haven't heard Julie mention her dad in years. To be honest, I thought she was shacking up with one of the janitors at that damn mall. Coming home later than usual. How she got all nervous when she mentioned Clay or when he was around. After I got moved over to Sunset, well, that probably sealed the deal. Things felt even more off with Jules." He rolled his eyes. "Police said they'd look into it. Then they have the nerve to tell me not to leave town!"

I kept a stone face while taking in his story, and more delicious coffee. "You worked with her?" Like I've said, playing dumb has benefits.

The young guard took a deep inhale. "Yeah. I did security at Mayview up until we lost the contract. Liked it better than this place, but there's definitely more activity here." His gaze drifted for a moment, the first flickers of joy I'd seen in the man.

"Why'd you guys lose the contract? Someone fumble on the play?"

"Fumble? Ha! That place was pretty much a ghost town compared to this. If I had to guess, that was the reason. Just not enough money coming in."

Another strike against dear Tiffany and her "thief" story.

"Be honest with me, man," Billy said. "What do you think is going on? Does it have something to do with... *the dead guy*?"

I caught a hint of disdain in his tone. "Weren't close with Mr. Cunningham?"

"Not really, but it's hard to believe the geezer is dead. Although it's not a surprise." His eyes darted around again.

"You seem a bit nervous, Billy."

He lowered his voice and leaned in. "You never know who's listening. Rumor is the old guy owed a ton of money and made a lot of enemies."

"Anyone in particular?"

"I don't like to listen to gossip, but I've heard everyone from the mayor to even Mr. Titus, the owner of Sunset. But if Jules was involved, I don't know what I'd do."

"Hi Billy!" a woman in her late twenties exclaimed as she walked by, adjusting her bright blue apron then walking behind the counter. The barista's yellow eyebrow ring matched the color of her bright gold wavy hair. He waved back and sank into the chair.

"Is that the other woman?" I asked, watching his face grow a few more tints pink.

"Jasmine's my favorite barista," he said, not catching my reference to the Ray Parker Jr. song about infidelity. You can't make it in this biz without having a finely tuned radar.

With more dead ends, two things were for sure: Tiffany had been playing me for a fool, and her late uncle had quite a few enemies. Time for a little chat with the ex-boss.

Chapter 22

I HAD MET my caffeine quota for the day, so I opted for an herbal tea. She was over twenty minutes late, but Mrs. Cunningham finally strolled through the doors of my favorite greasy spoon, fully decked out for mourning in her hip hugging black dress.

"Thanks for meeting with me." I motioned to the seat across. "Sorry again for your loss."

She hesitated over the table, not taking the invitation to sit.

"My husband said he already paid you. What is this about a new development that had to be in person? My family has gone through so much."

My next words planted her butt in the booth: "I know you're lying."

"Excuse me?" The black mod bucket hat popped off and fell on the table, sending a wave of messy copper strands across her face.

"I'm glad I have your attention." I took a sip from the mug, wishing it was filled with the coffee from the fancy mall. "Why did you hire me, Tiffany?"

She shifted in the plastic, making a crunch on the beat-up vinyl. "Um. The thefts. I needed your help." Using what little space there was, she smoothed out her dress. "To think my sister was capable of all of this." A deep, fake sigh of relief. "I should have known."

"Did you miss what I just said? I know you're lying. I've looked into it. Your old security company is singing a different tune. Nobody was stealing from you."

Another sigh from the woman, this time authentic. Her eyes caressed my chest, creating an uncomfortable shift of my own until realizing her intent.

"I'm not wearing a wire," I said. "Off the record. What the hell is going on?"

"Okay. You got me. You're a better detective than I thought." A seductive smile warped up her shimmering lips, the kind only a femme fatale from the nineties could. After a taste of her coffee, she pressed into the cushion. Her head swayed ever so slightly, bobbing to the sound of the Hall & Oates track playing quietly overhead. "I never lied to you, sweetie."

"Again, your former security detail says otherwise. You told me you dropped them after the thefts."

A snicker escaped while she traced the rim of the glass, now painted with a lip print reminding me of the old Pepsi Cool Cans. "And I did. I thought it may be an inside job. It wouldn't make much sense to tip anyone else off, would it? I told them we couldn't afford their services, which, as you can imagine from the lack of mall traffic these days, wasn't a stretch."

I hated to admit it, but it made sense. The line of questioning was flimsy at best. "So hiring the outside guy..."

"Exactly. You were supposed to be my fresh set of eyes. I had my suspicions about Debbie, but I hoped I was wrong."

If she was still lying, I would need more proof. Any hopes of tripping her up were fading, but I pressed on. "Something doesn't quite add up. I saw Debbie that night. She came looking for you. Something about a text saying to meet you at the office."

"I wanted to run a few business ideas by her before I left. But I got an urgent call from my husband about a water leak at the house. I didn't stick around."

She read my face and countered before I could speak. "Ask the cops. Plumber was at our place for hours."

"Okay. How'd your sister get in then? She didn't have keys to the door. I walked out with her."

A shrug from the lady in black. "I wish it weren't true more than anyone else. My sister, a thief and… murderer?"

"I don't know her well, but that doesn't seem like her."

"A killer? No, no it doesn't. I suppose you never truly know someone."

"What's her motive then?"

"All I can imagine is Uncle Robbie caught her in the act and she panicked. I'm sure we'll find out soon."

"I'd love to have a chat with her."

"Good luck. Her lawyer is keeping everyone away right now." A slight chuckle from the overdressed woman in grieving. "Odd how things turn out. To think I suspected Uncle Robbie of the thefts."

"Why's that?"

"He wanted to sell the mall, remember? Any way to make the numbers look even worse. Plus, he made some poor business deals, if you can call them that."

"Sounds like everyone in your family has their share of secrets. What's yours?"

Mascara filled lashes fluttered. "All this isn't enough? I'm busy keeping the mall afloat, detective. As I said, clearly I've underestimated your skill. You are thorough. I could appreciate that if I wasn't mourning my family and business collapsing before me."

She was right. Was I clouded here yet again? Laying it on thick while my former boss is going through hell? Geri would have slapped me if she saw this.

"I'm sorry. I wanted to tie up any loose ends."

"Thank you. Are we done here?"

I hesitated, vacillating between the fork in my thought process. "One more thing. Things were pretty chill for most of the night. Until a young lady came by. Do you know a Julie Carpenter?"

Now, your regular, average Joe wouldn't have thought anything of it. I'd imagine even some seasoned pros might overlook it too. But for the last few years, my bread and butter was cheaters. And the slight, barely noticeable quiver of the lip on little miss Tiffany was all I needed. To the rest of the world, they would be focused on her pupils, her cheek scrunching, and the shake of the head.

"Can't say I do. Hmm," she said. "The name seems vaguely familiar. A mall employee?"

"Yeah. I'm surprised the police didn't ask you about her. She showed up late that night to find her phone. I was with her the whole time."

"The detective woman may have mentioned something. I'm sorry. That night was a blur after I heard the news." She completely regained her composure. This woman was made of steel—no surprise she was well known in the Detroit business scene. "Now if you'll excuse me, I have a lot on my schedule as I believe you can appreciate. You are dedicated, I see that. But please just let this be. The local news harassment and police check-ins are enough. And since it wasn't said outright, the check you have yet to cash was our hope you wouldn't talk to the press and make this worse."

She stood, smoothing the unwrinkled dress once more, shooting an oddly seductive smile before walking away.

I sat in the diner long enough for the tea to grow cold, which I didn't mind. It actually tasted better with a chill.

Something still felt amiss. Tiffany had an answer to every question. Either she had a bulletproof fake story, or, like most people believed, she was telling the truth. But that Julie girl. Innocuous as the interaction was, the timing of her late-night visit was odd. Paired with Tiffany's reaction, I knew I had to find the punky girl—or figure out what happened to her. Julie's boyfriend had suspicions about a tryst with one of the janitors. And I knew just the man to call for help.

Chapter 23

"LET'S pretend it's a secret assignment. Deep uncover. Imagine you're Arnold in *True Lies*."

"Huh?" Bart said on the other end of the line.

"How about Jason Bourne?" I said, hoping to land a spy reference with the young man. "Bond?"

"Or maybe like *The Saint*?" Bart said excitedly, surprising this old guy with the mention of the Val Kilmer flick. Or was he referencing the classic Roger Moore TV show from the sixties?

"Yes!" I exclaimed, garnering the attention of another shopper in the drugstore aisle. I tempered my reaction, then pulled an iced tea from the fridge before walking to the self-checkout. "Exactly like the ole' Saint, buddy. Debbie really needs our help."

"Okay, I'll ask around and call you back as soon as possible. Over and out."

I laughed and pocketed the phone, scanning the chilly green tea over an invisible laser, pushing away intrusive thoughts of Skynet replacing humanity in the near future.

Back in my car, I chugged the minty tea and reclined the seat. *Just need a few seconds to rest my eyes.* Vision became hazy while harp music played through my speakers, or somewhere deep in my brain.

Decked out in a baggy orange prison jumpsuit, Debbie shuffled to the stainless steel table and sank onto the bench to face me. The room was filled with shadows and smelled like tea, probably the first sign I was dreaming. A guard leaned against the grey cracked wall with her arms crossed, the only other person in the room besides me and the woman in orange.

"Fancy meeting you here," I said, too jovial for the setting.

She avoided eye contact, head slightly craned toward the shiny metal table. "I hate that you're seeing me like this."

I shifted into a serious tone. "I'm glad your lawyer let me."

"They said you've been trying to help. Thank you." She looked up, eyes locking with mine. My chest tightened. Geri was right. I was smitten like a kitten.

"I know you didn't do it."

"No one else seems to think that." Her gaze drifted back to the metal. "My own sister won't even talk to me. Not that my lawyer wants me to, anyway. Everyone is saying I killed him. And that they found money in my locker."

"I was with you that night. Was anything out of the ordinary?"

"Everything was normal. Inventory, unboxing some new novels. Then I ran into you after that text from Tiff, and I went home."

"It didn't sound like she normally messages you."

"She would every now and again. More the past few weeks. Asking to stop by the office to talk about trivial mall business. I joked with Hakim that it was my version of office meetings about having meetings."

"What did the text say?"

"Nothing peculiar. Just to come to her office when I had a moment."

"And that's when I found you. You didn't have the keys. She was gone, so we walk out. That about it?"

"Yeah, I walked straight back to my car. Even waved goodbye to Bart, hanging out in his security car."

"See anyone else on the way out?"

We both paused, taking in the comforting sound of raindrops tapping against the steel roof above.

"No." She looked out at the iron-grated window. "I wish the cameras were working. My lawyer told me everything from that night was erased."

"Yeah. Convenient. So who do you think did this?"

She stood as the surrounding room darkened. A slight glow bathed her body, the light source unknown. "You're the detective. You were there. You already know. *Just unlock the door.* You can do that, can't you?"

A dangerously close crack of lightning startled me forward, smashing my forehead into the sun visor. Disoriented, I wiped my watery eyes, recovering focus on a lady in a red dress. The short woman scurried toward the drugstore, a newspaper shielding her head from the heavy rain. Thankfully, I had fixed my driver's side window last week. The last thing I needed was water pooling in. The six-minutes-too-fast clock in the DeLorean said I had either taken a short nap, or I just time traveled an hour into the future.

I still had plenty of daylight, but the running about town was clearly catching up. Not to mention last week's binge session of *Twin Peaks*—what would Dale Cooper take away from such a vision?

I tuned to the eighties station, having a slight shock from the song playing. "I can dream about you, if I can't hold you tonight..." *How about that for coincidence.*

The much welcome sound upgrade was the gift that kept on giving. Hopefully Bart would come through, I thought to myself. Seconds later, Crockett's theme replaced the Dan Hartman song.

"Sir, it's Bart," the voice blasted through my speakers.

"Tell me you've got something."

"Yes sir. Deep uncover, like you wanted. I got all the info you need, and more. I was able to confirm there were only two janitors at the mall that night. Mr. Clayton, the guy we ran into down in the maintenance room, and his roommate Forrest."

"Great, good work Bart."

"Thanks! But sir, I don't think either of them did it."

"Yeah? Why's that?" I said while starting the car.

"A, I saw both of them leave. Forrest earlier in the night, and I was with Clayton before he called his ride. They just seemed like their normal selves. Two, Clayton had double shoulder surgery within the year. He can still do his job, but Mr. Cunningham would always threaten to fire him because he was so limited. And D, Forrest is even older than his roommate. Like no offense, but he's been at the mall forever and he can barely move around. Takes him hours to clean the food court alone. Nice guy though."

I shook my head. "Good detective work. You get an address?"

"Sure did, 54 Lampkin Lane. Those apartments right off the I-75 service drive."

"A bit far from Haddonfield, aren't we?" I assumed the reference would go over the young man's head.

"Hey, *Halloween*! I love that movie!" The young officer was full of surprises.

Hopefully the janitors' place was more inviting than the old Myer's residence.

Chapter 24

LAMPKIN LANE WAS NESTLED DEEP in a row of apartments near street names based on Motown's greats. A right turn off of Four Tops Ave led to my destination, a small, two story block of townhouses. Despite being built over a decade ago, the buildings appeared well maintained. In fact, a cleaning crew was busy, blasting the vinyl siding with a fresh power wash and scrub.

Townhouse number fifty-four looked no different from the rest, aside from an extra row of potted plants on the porch, mostly daisies.

I used the shiny gold knocker and waited a moment on the freshly washed, soapy-smelling porch. The door soon opened to reveal a brightly lit living space behind Clayton, beaming a smile from ear to ear.

"Hey there!" the off-duty custodian said. "I was waiting for you. Come on in."

The warm welcome took me by surprise, but I appreciated skipping the formalities and getting down to business. I wondered what my secret agent told him.

"Bart said you had some questions about... that night." The long-haired man looked as if he was holding back a tear. "Have a seat. Can I get you something to drink?"

"No thanks," I said, sitting on the suede recliner. The inside had a faint smell of mothballs, adding to the brown and maroon theme. For the second time today, I had a memory of my grandma, helped by the vintage brown TV in the corner. Even decades later, I guess some aesthetics are hard to shake.

"Well then," Clayton said, easing himself onto the yellow fabric couch. "Police have asked plenty of questions, but I've been wondering when you'd come by."

His casual attitude was even more disarming than the greeting, not at all what I expected.

"Why's that?" I asked.

"There's a murder right after you're hired. You're not-so secretly a private eye. I suppose I didn't take you as a fella collecting a paycheck, riding off into the sunset as a mall cop."

"You got me," I chuckled. "So about that night..."

His jovial expression turned solemn. "I can't believe something like that could happen at Mayview."

"From what I heard, things weren't smooth sailing between you and Robert."

A faint snort of laughter from the older man. "We've had our disagreements, sure. In fact, I don't think we ever saw eye to eye on anything, other than hating reboots of movies. But I would never wish death on him. An accident like the one I had?" He pointed to one of his shoulders. "Sure, he could have used a lesson. But what happened to him? Nobody deserves that."

"What kind of accident did you have? Something at the mall?"

"You betcha. Last year, a pipe burst in the maintenance tunnels. Sent a big chunk'a steel into my chest. Don't ask me how, but it knocked into me so hard, broke both my shoulders and my hip."

"How's that even possible?"

"I said not to ask!" He howled, sitting up before wincing in pain. "Doc said the first hit probably shattered the left, then the fall broke the rest. Surgery wasn't as bad as the recovery."

This guy couldn't be that great of an actor—and I've seen my share of them. He was kind, cordial, and physically limited, probably living in chronic pain. Murderer, he was not. At least not capable of blunt force trauma, like in Uncle Robbie's case. The careful, shaky way he lifted his cup of water confirmed as much.

"Did you ever figure out why the pipe burst?" I asked.

"That's the thing, no. The insurance company sent a massive report filled with gobbledygook. The way my lawyer summed it up, they concluded poor working conditions. But if you ask me, I think someone tampered with it."

"Your lawyer? You sued?"

"Well, not exactly. It was Miss Debbie's idea. She found the attorney and everything. Robert didn't want to pay my hospital bill, even tried to fire me." He laughed again. "I know. It doesn't make me look very good right now, does it?"

It didn't, but I tried not to let it show. "I didn't say anything, Clay."

"Either way, they eventually paid my bills. Even got a nice little vacation to King's Island, although I didn't get to ride The Beast, of course. And in the end, I got to keep my job. Though Robbie never stopped complaining that I was too slow. That's why they got me the extra help at night."

I looked around the room, finding a few pictures of Clayton, some family, but none of his coworker and friend. "Speaking of, where is your roomie? Forrest was there with you that night, right? I ran into him." I imagined the old janitor singing tunes in the food court.

"Hmm. I'm surprised he didn't mention talking to you. It's Saturday right? His doctor is trying twice weekly dialysis to see how it goes. He was on three times a week before. Robert wasn't a huge fan of hiring back another old guy, but we take our time and have pride in our work."

One janitor that could barely raise his arms, and another on dialysis, both up there in age. Could they have knocked Robbie out? I suppose. But my gut said I was barking up the wrong tree.

"By any chance." I changed the subject. "Do you know a woman named Julie?"

The janitor's expression lit up like a Christmas tree. "Such a sweetheart. I haven't seen her in a few days, though. Why do you ask?"

"Her boyfriend is worried there's some funny business going on. And that she's seeing someone at the mall."

The man's forehead wrinkled. "We don't need any more bad news. She's such a sweet kid. Her boyfriend was always so protective. I was glad when he stopped working at the mall. Never liked him much."

"Why's that?"

"Always following me and the other guys around. I couldn't see Julie cheating, though. She's always been so nice to me and everyone else. Bringing donuts and coffee for the boys. That boyfriend of hers just takes me as the jealous type."

Clayton talked about the girl like she was his granddaughter. Stranger things have happened, but again, pulling from my extensive background, I didn't sniff any ounce of intimate interest within his words. Other than ruling out some suspects, this had been a total bust.

I stood up, disappointed by the lack of anything substantial in the case. As I was about to say goodbye, I blurted out the one question burning a hole in my noggin.

"One more thing," I said, fighting a sudden urge to straighten a crooked photo like Monk, another of my favorite TV detectives. "Why did you suspect foul play with the pipes?"

"A sixth sense, I guess." Clayton planted his feet carefully before standing, shuffling over to lead me to the door. "Nobody down in those tunnels but us cleaning boys. And Robert. He didn't know a wrench from a pair of pliers though, so I made peace with it and I told myself it was a freak accident."

"Why was Robert down there? These days it looked like he was living in the maintenance room."

"He was. But it didn't start that way. He was ducking that hotshot Titus, I think. Owed the guy a lot of money and people were getting tired of covering for him. Heck, even I lied for Rob a few times and said he wasn't at the mall. Gave him time to run around down there and disappear somehow."

"Interesting. Well Clayton, thanks for your time. And if you hear anything..." I flipped him my card before stomping down the steps.

The suspect list was dwindling, but so were my hopes of clearing Debbie's name. It was a longshot, but I had my next and only lead.

Chapter 25

TITUS HOLDINGS WAS LOCATED in the heart of downtown Detroit, nestled within one of the highrises in front of Campus Martius Park. In the winter, the sparsely treed park invited shoppers to explore dozens of tiny see-through huts lining the street, with local businesses selling everything from candles to cheese. And for the slightly more adventurous, a spin on the ice rink in the center of it all. Now in the first weeks of summer, the rink was replaced with a big sand pit and volleyball net. Although no one was playing, a few locals lounged in the beach chairs, jamming to the DJ spinning a smooth R&B track.

Inside the sleek, modern building, a fancy digital screen advertised Titus HQ—found on the 14th floor. A quick scan told it was one of a dozen businesses sharing space with a certain mortgage giant that owned the place.

"Can I help you, sir?" the bubbly secretary said.

At the welcome desk, I found a smiling young man. Sharply dressed in a tailored suit, his eyes matched the serene LED waterfall glistening behind. He was motionless with a locked gaze, waiting for a response.

In the distance, I eyed metal detectors and guards blocking the route to the elevators.

Now normally, I'd be full of all sorts of deception, using my Hollywood charm and improv skills to "yes, and" my way to the top. But I wasn't in the mood—it was getting late and the fleet of armed guards was out of my paygrade. So, I opted for the truth. "I'm here to see Mr. Titus."

"Ah yes. Titus Holdings, fourteenth floor." He tapped on his keyboard, squinting at the screen. "Hmm. Is he expecting you?"

"I've got a special delivery." Okay, I did have something up my sleeve, but it wasn't as elegant as a heist movie ruse.

The receptionist dubiously eyed my open arms. "A delivery, sir?"

I chuckled, watching him squirm until noticing we had caught a guard's attention. "Well, a verbal delivery. A message."

"Um. Okay," he said, followed by a few taps on his touchscreen. "I'll be sure to pass it along." His eyes returned to mine.

"This is," I paused, propping palms on the smooth desk to lean in closer. "A discrete matter." I flipped a business card from the ether and flung it his way, watching it land perfectly on his lap. I could only guess how closely the man knew Titus, seeing as he was the receptionist for the whole building, but I banked on the words *Intimacy Investigations* to add any needed pressure.

The shiny purple card did the trick—after a quick phone call, the young man spun back in his chair. "Mr. Titus will see you now. On the left through the metal detectors, Mr. Washington."

And to think, I almost stopped carrying the second version of my card. This was easy as pie, and I barely had to lie. A shame I missed out on using a fake pseudonym. Abe Froman, Nick Papagiorgio—I had a few ready in the chamber just itching to be used. Not many people caught the *Ferris Bueller* or *Vegas Vacation* references these days.

"Right this way, through the detector, Mr. Washington," said a well-dressed guard.

I walked through the steel poles without a hitch. No surprise—I hadn't carried a weapon since I played an evil henchman in a *Face/Off* clone. The decades-old movie was so laughably bad it should have been billed as a parody. Because of its tiny budget, instead of a prop gun I was packing the real deal—the director's own glove box Glock. *Remind me to never do that again.*

The elevator dinged a few times, stopping for an assortment of business-casual types before landing on floor fourteen. Seconds after the door opened, I was greeted by a tall, slender, part-time model that introduced herself as the assistant to Mr. Titus. She wasted no time leading me into a separate waiting room past several giant gold Ts—the company's gaudy logo. It was then I realized how prevalent the company really was, seeing their name on schools, apartment complexes, and even the new stadium being built a few miles away. I powered down the hallway, ignoring thoughts of *The Palace* implosion last year—and the heartache held for destroying my favorite childhood sporting arena.

"Have a seat please, Mr. Washington." The freckled brunette gestured to a leather couch facing a pair of rain-textured glass doors. "Mr. Titus will be with you shortly. Can I get you anything to drink?"

I broke my caffeine quota, not being one to skip a good time. Plus, a dig like this was sure to have something better than the instant coffee I had at home. Although I loved that grainy stuff, it brought me back to early college years of quiet breakfasts with mom.

The Katie Holmes look-alike did not disappoint. The coffee was delicious and crisp, rivaling the brew at the fancy mall. The magazine selection, however, was boring. I could only read so much about Metro Detroit's Top Docs before turning to my cell phone for entertainment.

I clicked on the screen to see I had missed a text.

> Hey bud. Got another batch of mail for you.
> Stop by the shop when you get a chance.

I was glad Corey put up with my constant flow of mail, and it was a good excuse to catch up. Adult friendships were harder to maintain, unless you get lucky and live across the hall like my sitcom neighbor Geri.

As if flung by another popular sitcom neighbor, a door blasted open to reveal an average height man, his black polo hastily tucked into too-tight blue jeans. Looking to be in his early sixties, I recognized the dark-complexioned man from the many pictures scattered throughout the brightly lit office.

"Well, what are you waiting for? Come on in!" Titus said, laughter in his voice while a smile accented his Germanic features.

Hesitant and thrown off by the cheery greeting, I cautiously followed the man into a small brown and red room. Ample windows illuminated the minimalist space, showing most of the many bookcases were filled with expensive looking relics. "Sit!" He ordered, still laughing as he sat at a tiny wooden desk, shutting a laptop in the process. "*Infidelity Investigations,* huh?" His expression changed from welcoming to serious, squinting and leaning into a high-back chair.

I approached the only other chair in the room, not fully putting my weight on the cushion at first. Titus was difficult to read, especially after the strange pleasantries—not what I expected after my unannounced visit and cryptic message to the receptionist.

It was soon clear he was used to taking control. Before I had a chance to respond, he continued, "the great thing about playing it safe is that you don't have anything to hide. Tell me why you're really here."

"For a guy that plays it safe, I'm surprised it was so easy to see you, a busy man as you are," I said with a bit of cockiness. It was the truth, though—the guy was easily a millionaire with a packed schedule, why humor me?

"You got me." He smiled and opened the laptop. "Playing hardball, huh? Let's see here." He scrolled the mouse wheel and clicked around for a few seconds too long. I zoned out, thinking about the detention in elementary school I got after stealing mouse balls from the computer lab. Some technology improvements are worth it—those mice would get filled with gunk.

Titus made one loud, final click and cleared his throat. "You're quite an interesting guy."

I wondered whether he was reading my wiki or the *Fangoria* article from a few years back, the latter being the first search result to come up from my name.

"Comes with the territory," I responded, keeping him on the offense.

"But what I really want to know, where did Cunningham hide it?"

Woah. That wasn't from my Wikipedia page. I'd bet that during those fifteen minutes in the waiting room, his cronies were snooping on their impromptu guest. Too bad I had no idea what he was talking about.

I played it *Cool as Ice,* the movie with the rapper that most people forgot. "Too bad we can't ask him. Maybe he left it somewhere in the *Hidden Temple,* next to the Shrine of the Silver Monkey."

"You've got five minutes. And save the millennial jokes for your little newspaper article." He was even less jovial, no signs of the happy guy that greeted me. "Cunningham was dodging me for weeks. I've seen the local news. I'm aware you were working at his mall. I don't know who you're with now, but I'll pay double if you can find it."

My acting chops had helped prepare me for this moment, not reacting to his bombshell of a statement. *What was he looking for?*

"An interesting proposition," I said, briefly drumming against the arms of the chair. That wasn't part of the act—I was confused as all get out, but I didn't want to clue the businessman in. "How did you know I was looking for it?" I took a shot in the dark, nothing to lose but looking like a fool in front of one of the city's most powerful men.

"Don't play with me. You abruptly take a break from snooping on petty liars, to start working at a failing mall. *Coincidentally* the same month Robert gets his hands on my painting? Not to mention he shows up dead days later." He showed a slight tinge of nervousness as his hands went out of view under his desk. "Your work? Doesn't seem like your style."

Of course, I find myself in a *Maltese Falcon* type situation. My macguffin, a painting. A shiver of electricity danced down my spine at the thought of being part of a deeper mystery.

"Murders not my bag, baby," I said, without the *Austin Powers* accent. "I prefer sticking to the shadows. But from what I hear, you've been trying to find him for a while now." *That,* I recently learned.

"Damn straight I have. But murder isn't my game, either. And it wouldn't help me much. I gave the guy thousands to broker the deal. And before you say anything, this is all on the up and up. That piece of artwork has been in my family for years. Until it was stolen during the war. Finally, I heard it was floating around on the black market, and of course, only Cunningham has the connection." He stopped to shake his head. "But you already knew that, didn't you?"

I sure didn't, but he didn't need to know that. "Well, if your sources didn't tell you, I'm off the mall job. Axed after they found his body."

His hands reappeared, clasped together on the desk. "Do you have it already?"

"No, but if I find it, you'll be the first to know." Hollywood royalties were alright, but reuniting a man with his family art, *and a big payday,* now that was a hard offer to turn down.

"Then why are you here?" He looked as confused as I felt.

"Art aside, let's say I don't think Robert's niece was the one to give him the big sleep." I was definitely feeling my noir self right now.

"So that's your angle? Interesting family, watch your back. That painting has more than a few fans. And Cunningham had quite a reputation. He left this earth with enough debt to put me in the red." He laughed. "Well, not that much, but it was hefty. Bring it to me, and you'll be glad you did."

The sales pitch was good, and a cash bonus would be great, but a vision of Debbie in orange reminded me of priority number one. As cute as she looked, I needed to get her out of there. The painting would have to wait. *Unless she had something to do with it.*

"Say," I said, crossing my arms with force hoping to disarm him. "You're a busy guy. Why did you stop by so many times to see Robert? You could have just sent someone."

"And I did. My men kept getting lost, chasing him in those tunnels underneath the mall. Somehow he always seemed to sneak away." The man shook his head. "Robert was a friend, once. I hoped I could talk reason into him, face to face. But whenever I showed up, the same thing… gone. Even with my team watching the place."

The meeting ended as oddly as it began, with Titus taking a call and rushing me out the door.

And here I was—countless interviews, a missing girl, and dead end leads—no further than I started. The longer Debbie lingered in a cell, the further her freedom felt. With the moon in full view and the city beginning its descent into a weekend slumber, I decided to attack tomorrow with a fresh head.

Chapter 26

BRIGHT AND EARLY, I marched into the pawnshop, filled with enough coffee to satisfy all the *Friends* at Central Perk. It was needed—a rare night of tossing and turning meant my razor sharp focus was as dull as the replica *Highlander* sword above the door. *So much for a fresh head.*

"You look like hell," my all-too-honest friend greeted. "Rough night?"

"I barely got any sleep. I woke up every half hour. Even tried watching some Letterman reruns. No dice." The old *Late Show* was a favorite, although it almost always sent me snoozing.

"Well, I got some light reading for you. Here ya go." Corey dropped a large bundle of papers on the glass countertop. "Most of em are letters, along with the usual assortment of credit card offers. Three times the usual."

"Better than AOL CDs," I said, thumbing through the assortment of mail. "I'm quite the popular guy. Five letters? I forgot the fan club P.O. Box still forwarded here."

"I'll bet it's because they mentioned you on the local news."

I stopped sorting, pausing to take a step back away from the pawnshop counter. "What's that now?"

Corey laughed, shifting on his barstool, tapping the old-timey 1920s register. "Had your picture up there and everything. Something like..." He cleared his throat and mimicked his best newscaster impersonation, *"Metro Detroit's very own actor-turned-investigator, Paul Washington, has been linked to the investigation."*

"Great. I saw a news van circling the mall. I was hoping they didn't spot me. Maybe someone slipped my name. At least now I know whose calls I've been ignoring." I stole a glance at a suspicious-looking guy in a fedora, leaning on the jewelry counter across the shop. I dropped the paranoia, reminding myself most of Corey's customers were suspicious—present company included. "Did they at least use a good picture?"

"Yeah actually. A headshot from that photoshoot you did a few years ago. The girl *really* into yoga. The one where you—"

"Don't remind me. She took forever to send the pictures, and I paid double in the end."

"At least they turned out good." Corey spun in his seat and grabbed a cardboard box, then dropped it on the counter. "Speaking of reminding, I just got a batch of comic books in. Wow, nice!" He pulled out a *Sonic the Hedgehog* book from the early Archie era. "So anyway, how *is* that mall investigation going?"

I debated mentioning the painting side-quest, but I wasn't in the mood for a game of 21 questions from my old art-loving friend. Instead, I stuck to a concise summary, hustling around the city with not much to show for it, ending on Mr. Titus' own dead end in the secret mall tunnels.

"Of course he couldn't catch him," Corey said matter-of-factly. "I remember hearing my friends getting lost down there for hours."

"The way you talk about those tunnels makes them sound legendary."

"They were, or so I heard. Rumor was they extended past the mall's parking lot. Like secret entrances and exits to the place. A guy I worked with back then said he wandered down there and found stairs that led outside, came out of a little utility hut over by the old Sizzler." He chuckled and shook his head. "I remember checking it out a few weeks later, nada. He swore they bulldozed it. He did like to tell some tall tales."

My eyes widened. "No chance he was telling the truth?"

"I always left room for doubt. The idea of a secret maze under the mall was just way too cool. And I've heard stories of college campuses and airports having complex underground systems."

I tapped a finger against my cheek, digesting the theory and what seemed like the first real break in the case. "So if your friend's story *was* true, not only could Robbie use it to run from his debtors..."

"Your murderer could have used them, too," Corey finished my thought, enthusiasm in his voice. He quickly regained his composure in a measured tone. "That is, if your girlfriend didn't do it."

"I know she didn't. I have to get back down there, but I'm not exactly on the mall's guest list." I tapped on the glass, wheels turning in my brain. "If any of these secret entrances still exist, I might be closer to proving Debbie is innocent."

"It would be really cool if any were intact. I've seen videos online of malls having fully preserved fast-food restaurants behind maintenance doors. Some even covered by loose drywall for decades!" He took a deep, zen-like breath. "But what if they built over them already? We're talking well over forty years here, bud. Maybe he was really good at hide and seek?"

"I gotta go with my gut here. There's something to those tunnels." I collected the mail and shoved it under my arm. "Besides, my schedule is clear. What's the worst that could happen?" I smiled.

"Not so fast, space ace. How exactly do you think you're gonna get down there? Randomly drive around and look for a secret door or false wall? This isn't a video game. You're going to need the blueprints or something."

Little did Corey know, that was already on my mind. What better place to learn about my city than the public library? While most information could be found with a quick search, the old stuff was buried away in deep storage, hidden in cold basements on microfiche, never seeing a ray of sunlight. Or the digitization process—making my journey below the library feel even more special.

"Right this way," the freckle-faced librarian said. The cheery woman wore the excessively large keyring as a bracelet, jangling through the hall like Santa was coming. "We don't get many visitors to this place. I'm glad we didn't file these keys away yet. Last time it took a week to find em." She fumbled at the door, trying a few keys until we heard a satisfying click.

I paused before entering the records room. "You had another visitor?"

"Earlier this week. One of the girls had a guy wanting to look up some articles from the seventies."

My eyebrows raised. *That can't be a coincidence.*

I feigned casual curiosity. "Oh yeah? What was he looking into?"

"I think she said he was researching the park across the street. Something about birds and migration patterns."

She shrugged and flipped a switch in the tiny room. Two small lamps flickered before settling, providing barely enough light to see a microfiche reader pressed against the cracked brick wall. The giant white and grey boxy thing looked like an oversized Apple II from my elementary computer classes.

"Wow. Can you play *Oregon Trail* on this thing?" I asked.

The young woman shrugged and hunched over to power on the screen. "Sorry it's so cramped. We moved this down here a while back since it's barely used. Until now, I guess!"

A low hum buzzed from the plastic and steel gateway to the past. I stood back, expecting it to start vibrating and shoot out a plume of smoke. Instead, a pale blue glow filled the room, the grainy blank display coming to life.

"Well, there ya go!" The woman began to turn toward the hall.

"One more question." I approached the obsolete relic of history. "How do I use this?"

The redhead turned and chuckled. "Oh, I'm sorry. One track mind! When my boss said you needed to use this, well, nevermind —you need a slide to see anything. This ole beast is only a reader." She continued out the door. "Follow me, across the hall."

My guide opened the door marked *Special Collections,* leading us into another dark, dusty room. This one was much larger, filled with rows of filing cabinets, some steel, some wood. I scanned the labels, finding 1961 as the earliest date on the faded label cards.

"How are these organized?" I asked. "Dewey Decimal?"

The librarian laughed again. Either I was really that funny, or her day was really slow. "No, not for microfiche. Those will be in the metal cabinets over there, arranged by date and category. What were you looking for again?"

I made a beeline for the steel drawer labeled *Blueprints*. "Bingo." It slid open much easier than I would have guessed.

"Looks like you've got this," she said. "I'll be upstairs. Just come find me when you're done. And remember, nothing in here can be rented or removed."

And just like that, I was alone in the creepiest part of the library. I wasn't one to scare easily, but after seeing the opening scene of *Ghostbusters* when I was six, well, library trips were never the same. That ghostly librarian still gave me chills.

I regained my focus and thumbed through dozens of thin sleeves, the little plastic postcards neatly arranged in alphabetical order. City Hall, Police Station, Subdivisions. I scanned through the list twice. No trace of Mayview Mall. Before ending my mission, I remembered the original name for the shopping center when it first opened: Lakeview. Back to the Ls and... empty. And not just empty as in not there—the clear lack of dust in the empty slot was all I needed to see. Someone had taken the microfiche.

I shook my head in anger. "*Birds, huh....*" Someone beat me to it, and I had a strong suspicion it was a recent avian-loving rule breaker. Before slamming the drawer in frustration and running up the stairs like the halls of my high school, I paused, eying the row of cabinets storing old issues of the local newspaper. *An extra five minutes won't hurt.*

The poor basement reception huffed and puffed, struggling to find the results of my search: Lakeview Mall opened in the Fall of 1976, rebranding to Mayview a few months later. I rifled through the seventies drawer, curious to see if it held any interesting articles related to the childhood rumors. And just as before, a few key slides were missing—these, however, were filled with enough dust to show they were taken long ago. Or never existed. Curiosity be damned—the early days of the mall would remain a mystery.

Back upstairs, I found the giggly ginger bookkeeper sorting new releases, who instantly saw the look on my face. "No luck, huh?"

"The search continues," I said. "Say, you mentioned someone else visiting recently..."

She cautiously lowered her book—the latest cash-in autobiography from an actor I had some beef with, in another life.

"I did..." She paused, pursing her lips tightly before continuing. "Why do you ask?"

"Well, I'm part of an old Detroit history group." The lie slithered out, an unfortunate common occurrence for this private eye, although the fake group sounded cool. "You wouldn't happen to remember who stopped by, would you? I was wondering if it was my friend, Teddy." I held back adding the last name of my favorite talking bear: Ruxpin.

"This wouldn't have anything to do with the murder at the mall, right? I recognized you after I went upstairs, *Mr. Burke,*" she added an icy emphasis to remind me of the pseudonym I gave her, the perfect reaction for everyone's favorite jerk that turned on Ripley in *Aliens*.

"I try to keep a low profile—"

There was no sign of the gentle librarian from before as her sharp words cut through. "I don't appreciate being lied to, mister."

"I'm sorry." I stirred up the biggest puppy dog face I could muster. "That news story has really got me on edge." Hopefully playing the sympathy card would do the trick.

"The library is serious business," she said, then paused to take a deep breath. "Next time, just be honest, okay?"

I nodded, my body reacting like I had received a scolding from the middle school librarian Mrs. Hancock after browsing eBay in computer class. "Yes ma'am!" I blurted out.

Her expression reverted to the warmth of the initial greeting. "Good." She uncrossed her arms. "As for your friend, *if any of that was even true,* you'll have to ask Barb. I wasn't here that day." She pointed to a grey-haired woman with large glasses scanning books for a young reader.

Barb was just as kind as her coworker, the version that didn't catch me in a lie, that is. "Hello, young man. Say, you look familiar."

"I get that all the time." I smiled, putting my hands on the reception desk.

She looked down with a flicker of annoyance at my fingers resting on the clean wood table. "How can I help you?"

"I was just in special collections," I pointed a thumb over my shoulder, no idea if that was the right direction. "That very kind young lady mentioned you helped someone down there recently."

Her eyes narrowed with suspicion, not quite as heavy as her redheaded colleague. "That I did. Not many guests ask to go down there these days."

"Did you get their name? I'm working on a project and I'm worried we're doubling our work!"

She looked at my fingers again, causing me to recoil and pocket my hands. "No, sorry I didn't." Her eyes darted to a patron waiting to check out. "Now, unless there's anything else..."

"One more thing. Do you remember what they looked like?"

More annoyance from the lady. I should have pretended to borrow a book. "Handsome young black man. Style was a bit garish if you ask me. Looked like he stepped out of a time machine."

"Thank you for your time." I nodded, knowing exactly where to head next.

Chapter 27

I OPTED to park on the street a block from Robust Robin. The last thing I wanted was to announce my arrival or deal with their security. Plus, I had plenty of questions for Alan—the less he could prepare, the better.

With the uptick in virtual meetings, in some ways my job became a whole lot harder. Pre-zoom and FaceTime, a private eye had a higher chance of spotting a shady business transaction. Ducking behind dumpsters, sneaking around alleyways—being a private eye in the eighties and nineties sounded so much more fun —not to mention dangerous. Now, you're lucky to spot an illicit meeting, the rare times they actually happen in person. So when I saw Mr. Titus himself sauntering out of the security HQ, I hit the jackpot.

I watched as the businessman drove off in his gaudy, expensive car. Either Titus wasn't as busy as I thought, or he had a really good reason to meet face to face. And in my line of work, that's usually dodging eavesdropping ears on a recording device. *What was he up to?*

I hopped out of the car and took a stroll over the cracked sidewalk, past the closed businesses. Soon, the pavement turned pristine, leading to the quaint little area Robust Robin had claimed as its own. A few more of these little businesses and the street would be a lot more inviting. I had to give Alan that.

I pushed open the ultra-clean glass door and stomped into the lobby with purpose. Seeing Titus had both thrown me off and ignited an excitement, adding more fuel to the energy I brought to the receptionist. Surprised, she squirmed and nervously eyed her surroundings. I eased on my power walk and shot her a smile, approaching the desk.

"Alan in?" I said, adding a bit of charm to offset the tension.

She cleared her throat, then clutched her stringy necklace before speaking. "I, ugh, don't believe he has you on his schedule, sir."

"Surprise visit. Tell him I've got a brand new set of pogs he's gonna love. Birds of America collection."

As expected, the receptionist had no idea what pogs were. Instead of explaining the strange game of slamming cardboard circles, I pressed her to call the boss. What followed was an awkward conversation of the woman repeating herself until I urged an emphasis on the word *birds*. Seconds later, the owner appeared, leaning against the railing overlooking the lobby.

"I've been expecting you." He gestured to the stairs. "Come on up."

After a wink at the confused woman, I climbed the stairs toward the neatly dressed man. Today's outfit was a navy blue pinstripe suit, a baby blue button up underneath. I would have to get the number of his stylist.

"Welcome back, Washington." My well-dressed rival extended his hand for a handshake. I obliged, curious to see where this was going to lead. "Come in on."

Inside the fishbowl, the once immaculate executive table was littered with papers and diagrams. Blown up replicas swayed in the breeze, taped to a whiteboard in the corner. Even through the multi-colored markup and scribbled notes, it was clear what I was looking at.

"How'd you know I was coming?" I said, crossing my arms.

Alan joined me at the whiteboard, standing shoulder to shoulder. We stood in silence for a beat, looking over the blueprints. "I don't hire idiots, Washington," he finally said. "I'm actually glad you're here. It proves my instincts are still sharp. Offer still stands to join."

I ignored the proposal. "Nice story about the birds. Those librarians aren't going to be too happy you took this."

"Borrowed." He turned to offer a smile. "Don't bother snitching. They won't mind after the donation comes their way."

"Titus."

He shook his head. "I told the old fool to be more discreet."

I pointed to the blueprint. "Doesn't he own Sunset Mall? What does he want with Mayview?" Feigning ignorance was often a gamble, but with the offer Titus threw at me, I doubted Alan knew of the rich man's offer.

The other private eye laughed, finding his way to a leather chair at the table. "He owns a quarter of Metro Detroit, give or take a few percent."

"You're not answering the question."

"Stop stacking your questions. It makes them easier to dodge."

I sighed. There was a reason I was the number two in town, but to be fair, I've only been at this professionally for a few years.

"Robert's dead and you've stolen the blueprints to his mall," I said with the most seriousness I could muster. "This doesn't look good."

"You don't see me hiding them, do you? Remember, I invited you up here. I could ask the same question back to you."

"Now who's stacking the questions!" I said, immediately realizing how foolish it sounded. "Anyway, what's he want with the mall?

"Our interests are aligned, Washington."

"I'm trying to find Robert's killer. And right now, your boss doesn't look clean. Did he kill him?"

Alan stood and walked back to the board. "No. Titus was clear not to hurt the man. Robert was hiding something from him. Something that got him killed." He tapped on the blueprint. "I have a feeling it's somewhere in there."

"In your whiteboard?"

Alan shot a smirk over his shoulder. "Funny." He turned to the map. "As you're already aware, there's a whole maze under Mayview. Deep enough to store valuables, or in your case, make a clean getaway."

"You think they got the wrong girl, too?"

"Not my concern. But I know she doesn't have what I want. So I'm willing to share if you are." He waved a hand over the board then rubbed his chin. "You get access to the blueprints to try to clear her name. And I get first dibs on the item *I'm looking for*. Well, only dibs."

The item. Alan was careful not to give too much information. That all but confirmed he didn't know I was in the loop about the painting. While Titus's money could give me a massive boost toward building the personal pop culture museum I fantasized about, I knew some things could wait.

"Deal," I said. "So now that we're sharing, how do you know Debbie doesn't have this item?"

"I've had eyes on that family for weeks. And before you ask, no, I don't have any hard proof she's innocent."

"What about implicating someone else? You must have some theories."

"I'll be honest. After we lost the Mayview contract, our access was severely reduced. All signs point to there being another player in town." He paused, running a finger across the enlarged map, tracing an outline of the mall. "Hopefully it's not too late."

Mr. Number One with no suspects for his case? I still had plenty for mine. Julie. Maybe her boyfriend. I suppose Tiffany or her husband, Wyatt. Mr. Titus. Hell, even Alan could have done it. And I ruled some out. The janitors and Bart were on my side. *I think.*

I tilted my head slightly, studying the board again. "Okay then, what's with the color coding you've added to that map of yours?"

"A list of the entrances and exits... and dead ends. These green markers represent every publicly accessible entrance to the mall.

You were already looking for the blueprints, so I'll assume you knew of the unmarked access points. Blue over here, those two are auxiliary doors that lead from the maintenance tunnels to the outside."

I couldn't hold back the burst of joy and let out an audible squeal. "Yes!" I took a short breath. "The killer used those to sneak in and out without a trace?"

"Cool down, hot shot." Alan let out the tiniest bit of air. "You wouldn't be standing here if it were that easy. I'm still the best in town, remember?" I rolled my eyes while he continued. "I tried pulling the camera footage from the mall, but—"

I finished his sentence. "Someone tampered with the feed."

"Right. So I got the next best thing. Security footage from the big box wine store and Middle Eastern restaurant, here..." He pressed into the whiteboard with enough force to push it back an inch. "And here. The good news, we have surprisingly clear views of the area. The bad news, they show nothing out of the usual. Another brick wall, literally and figuratively."

I was impressed. I assured myself I would have thought of the same thing and was grateful Alan hit fast forward on a few days of work. "Okay, then what are these red X's?"

"Those three are the real dead ends. According to the original blueprints, those mall tunnels had exits that ran quite a way from the main building. These two here are pure stops. One recently had a strip mall built over it, and the other is a parking spot. It must have been completely paved over."

I thought of Corey's story. He would love confirmation that the rumor was true.

"And the last one, here?" I circled the area with a finger. "It looks like it's almost a mile from the mall."

"A little over a kilometer. And more of the same, unfortunately."

"Paved over?"

"Worse, they built a steakhouse above it. It's been abandoned for years."

I ran a finger down my temple to meet my chin, tapping while the wheels cranked away upstairs. The lightbulb eventually flickered, brighter than the neons in Geri's apartment.

"You haven't taken a peek inside, have you?" I asked.

Alan's expression was a mix of disappointment and curiosity.

"Well," I said. "I'm feeling like chicken tonight. Also steak, definitely steak."

Chapter 28

"HEY, WHAT DID THOSE KIDS WANT?" Alan asked.

I jogged to meet him as he circled the abandoned Sizzler. "Just wanted the autograph of Detroit's best detective, is all."

"Are you sure they weren't fans of your crappy late night movies?" He snickered. "Hey, check that out." He pointed to the back entrance, chained together and secured with a small padlock.

The back of the restaurant matched the front: weeds pushed through cracks in the pavement, the walls lined with pink graffiti tags on individual bricks. A gritty layer of dirt covered the windows—the place had seen better days. I hoped we could turn this red X into blue on Alan's map, but it didn't look like the building had seen a soul in years. Even urban explorers probably passed it up, opting to wander in abandoned amusement parks instead. Luckily, the steakhouse was small enough and had a decent roof, so the concerns of still water or dead air were minimal.

"Can you pick a lock?" Alan said with a smile curving from cheek to cheek.

"What P.I. doesn't know how to pick a lock?" I studied the chain. "This one looks recent. I'd expect to find more rust and wear. Someone's used it within a year, at the very least."

"Great minds think alike." He pulled a black leather case from his coat pocket. "Want to do the honors?"

I eyed the lock picks before shooting a glance at my rival. "Just get it open."

He scoffed, and within seconds, his fast hands danced around the doorknob. The chain and padlock dropped to the ground. I hid my shock—he was fast. Quicker than me. I guess the title of number one was appropriate, at least in this case.

He pulled the heavy door, creaking and grinding against the uneven cement. "Age before beauty," he said, with an extended hand.

I hated that saying, but in this case, it was probably accurate. I had a good three or four years on the man, and if we're talking about his style, I already made my jealousy clear.

The inside of the steakhouse was dark, cool, and clammy.

"Keep an eye for any signs someone was here," Alan said.

The door closed behind—with it, taking most of the natural light from the setting sun outside. Left in darkness, the boarded-up windows only gave slivers of light to guide our way. A shiver shot down my neck, either from a gust of wind or a ghost warning of impending doom.

A corner of the restaurant lit up with a click. "You remember your flashlight?" Alan's voice echoed from several feet away.

"Who needs flashlights when you have a phone?" I tapped a few buttons and cast a beam of light from my cell, ignoring his attempt to catch me unprepared.

Alan whistled quietly. "Wow, this is in better shape than I predicted."

Having been in my fair share of abandoned businesses, I didn't share his surprise. Some closed shops were well preserved—several even appearing as they were only closed for days, not decades. Well, aside from the layers of dust and dated beverage selection. I spied a fountain drink dispenser behind the bar, the green Surge logo prominently on display.

I lowered my digital torch, illuminating a few areas of wet, moldy carpet. "Check this out." I cast the light on a set of muddy shoe prints leading away from the pool.

Alan inspected the print. "Looks recent. Men's boot. Around size ten."

I took charge, following the path. "Look, it leads this way." I pointed the light on the gradually fading footprints. "Ends here at the bar."

My temporary partner cautiously crept around the bartop, scanning the ground. I opted to leap, propping myself up and over the counter, landing with a not-so-grateful crash on the other side.

"Washington! What the—"

"I always wanted to do that." I beamed a smile in the darkness.

"Be careful! And quiet. It looks like the trail goes cold. Look for anything out of place."

"Thanks for the advice, *dick*." He was great at pointing out the obvious. Was I this annoying to other people? "As far as I'm concerned, the only thing out of place here is us. We should be looking for anything that looks new."

I caught a glimpse of Alan's face under a slice of moonlight, the look of annoyance. He knew I was right.

We snuck through the steakhouse carefully. Booths waited longingly for patrons that would never return, some even set with menus or silverware. The bar was mostly empty, although a few bottles of half-full whisky lined the mirrored backing. Walls were covered with pictures, most still intact—local sports teams and memorabilia mixed with pictures of action stars from the nineties. Signed headshots of Ted Danson and Steven Seagal took center stage above where the maitre'd would stand, the most pleasant of greetings for hungry guests. I debated taking a few of the items for my new office.

"Don't even think about it," Alan said, reading the conflict on my face. "You find anything worthwhile? Other than all this retro stuff."

"I'll pretend I didn't hear that. This is more than just stuff. I would have figured you'd love this."

"Who said I didn't? I'm all business right now. You know, my group could teach you a thing or two."

"I prefer being my own boss, thank you very much." A glimmer in the corner caught my eye. "Hey, what's that over there?" I focused my light toward the shimmer in the distance.

Alan's light joined to reveal one of the double doors to the kitchen swaying, just enough to cast a reflection as it swung from the invisible breeze. "This place gives me the creeps."

"Detroit's top detective scared by an old restaurant? C'mon!" I strutted toward the kitchen until the biggest rat I'd ever seen scurried across my sneakers. I leapt back with an audible gasp, tripping over the wet floor sign doing a poor job warning of the soggy floor.

Alan doubled over laughing, shaking his head without saying a word.

"Consider us even," I said, pushing one of the swing doors open. "I love rats, by the way. You see the size of that thing? I think it was a chupacabra."

"Of course it was," Alan said, barely holding back his laughter. "This is a dirty game. A little fear isn't bad for us. Keeps us..." he paused, the flashlight uncovering a prep table littered with an assortment of knives. "Alive."

My counterpart approached the stainless steel table and inspected the cutlery, then turned to an oversized oven covered in cobwebs. I headed in the opposite direction, dodging an open can of dried pasta sauce and several spice bottles along the way. Glass crunched under my feet, my phone illuminating a pathway of broken wine bottles with dry red vino caked on the tile floor. I passed an industrial meat slicer, gauging from the rust and webbing, it hadn't seen a slice of meat in over a decade. Peeling paint melded with blocks of enough mold to make me wonder if we should be wearing protective gear.

"How's it going over there?" Alan shouted from the other end of the kitchen.

"Great!" I said, holding up a spatula from the counter.

"Funny guy. If there's a secret entrance to the tunnels, I'm not seeing it."

"Giving up so easily?" I said, while playing the real-life version of *Minesweeper* on the way to the walk-in refrigerator. "We still need to check this out." I yanked open the heavy door and looked over my shoulder. "Grab something to prop this thing open. I don't wanna get stuck here like in that *Punky Brewster* episode."

After using a heavy jug of expired butter to secure the door—and soothe my inner child—we entered the large fridge. The smell hit us at the same time, both recoiling from the sour sewage fumes wafting from the floor drain.

"Let's make this quick," Alan said, covering his mouth with the collar of his jacket.

I pinched my nose and scanned the oversized cooler, only finding moldy, cracked plastic walls lined with empty steel racks. My sharply dressed partner was of no help, fighting a coughing fit.

He regained his composure and leaned against a wobbly storage rack. "More dust than a haunted house. Layers of it. Are you thinking what I'm thinking?"

"Probably not. I'm wondering how many of those celebrity 8x10s I can carry out."

"The only thing we're going to leave with is a brain eating amoeba." He turned and left me alone in the walk-in.

Even as I was losing momentum, *and fresh air,* my gut told me to keep looking. Or maybe it was the rancid chemicals scrambling my thoughts. Either way, my light passed the grease lined tiles near the racks until... "Wait!" I shouted.

In front of the furthest metal shelving unit, the ground was scuffed and torn.

"Check this out," I said, focusing the light on the floor. "Less dust in front of this one. Ground is shredded. This rack has been pulled out. A lot."

Alan hobbled in with a few more coughs, then knelt near the

shelf. "Well, I'll be." He looked back with a smirk, shaking his head. "How did you…"

"I don't know. I'm making this up as I go," I said with the tip of an imaginary fedora, a nod to the fabled Dr. Jones. "Let's see what's behind this thing."

I grabbed the middle while Alan used his position on the ground to pull the rack from the wall. While I was no stranger to heavy weights, my partner was clearly friends with the iron—he did most of the work. The shelf screeched a horrid groan during its journey until we both took a break, inspecting the wall behind. We shot each other a look before our eyes went back to the faint outline of what had to be a secret passageway.

"WELL, I'LL BE," Alan repeated himself.

"You'll be what?" I laughed. "I told you we'd find something. That's gotta be it."

Alan walked to the textured plastic wall, tracing the outline without touching it. I appreciated his careful approach, but the glee of finding a secret door in an abandoned building was too much to contain. Gently pushing him aside, I pressed a palm in the center of the panel, finding it flimsy, but strong enough to take the pressure. Without hesitation, I jogged back into the kitchen, snatched a thick butcher's knife from a prep table, and carefully made my way back into the cooler.

"Woah!" Alan yelled while backing into a corner of the walk-in.

I ignored his surprise and jammed the tip of the blade under a faintly visible crack in the wall, prying at it with a fair amount of leverage. The panel popped open to reveal pure darkness and a waft of stale, acrid air. "One, two, three, not it!" I said with the quickness, not giving Alan a chance to rebut.

He rolled his eyes. "Sure you don't want to do rock, paper, scissors instead?"

"You're the number one detective, after you." I waved him in with my cellphone flashlight like I was on an airport landing strip.

He apprehensively stepped into the large opening, beaming his light from top to bottom. "Ha, check out this wall."

In the tight corridor, his light revealed the words *Chi-Chi's* with a few names inscribed under the logo on the brick wall.

"Ah memories," I said. Visions of a birthday party at the old Mexican restaurant drifted by like the musty breeze. If it weren't for the stinky secret tunnel, I might have been able to recall the aroma of the delicious salsa and chips. "I almost forgot it used to be here, in the nineties before the Sizzler."

"Well, aren't you special? Keep moving."

A few seconds later, my guide stopped, focusing his light on a set of steps leading down, opening into a slightly larger room. A few empty boxes lay scattered in the darkness. I imagined this being an extra storage room decades ago, or a place where the cooks would hang out for a break. A few more feet away, the other side opened to another dip below. We carefully trotted down the steps, these being a proper staircase descending quite a bit. Alan slipped on a slick step, testing his core strength and the durability of the old steel railing.

I guessed we were now deep underneath the restaurant's parking lot. Excitement coursed within, the thought that we were part of an exclusive club that had explored this area—some of the first in years, or maybe even decades—adding to the thrill.

The staircase ended, presenting us with a dead end and a quick ninety-degree turn. We followed the brick-lined tunnel and were greeted by rusty iron bars, more brown than the original black coating. Alan pushed against the metal. To his surprise, it swung easily, albeit loudly, granting us entry to the rest of the dark corridor.

"You forgetting something?" I said, before mocking his overuse of "Well, I'll be."

After a quick retort, we resumed our trek for several minutes. Again, I attempted to visualize our position in the tunnel compared to the world above. I placed us at the ascent to the old Sears entrance that was now shuttered. Or I was completely wrong and we were bumbling further from the mall, in for a giant surprise. Maybe we'd pop out of the ground from a manhole in the middle of the street like a set of mutant turtles. I imagined my confused sidekick dodging cars like he was playing the arcade classic, *Frogger*.

"What's so funny back there?" Alan said.

"Oh nothing. Never thought I'd be linking up with you, that's all."

"Oh yeah? I figured you'd be all for reliving those buddy cop movies, being obsessed with the past and all."

"You've really read my columns, huh?"

"I wouldn't try to hire you without doing my research. I'm surprised you haven't made any *Men in Black* references yet."

"There's time." I chuckled. "And *Rush Hour* was more my speed. But that would mean you're my partner. And I was hoping my first homicide case would be solo."

I slowed as my wannabe boss approached another steel barrier, this one ajar. He pressed a shoulder into the unforgiving bars, the obstruction not complying with his attempt. "Give me a hand here."

I fought the urge to give a round of applause and grabbed the iron door. We pushed and pressed until deciding it was futile—the door was solidly fused with the concrete, giving little space for anyone to eek through.

"Hmm." Alan studied the opening. "Not much room here to get anything out..."

"I was thinking the same thing. Probably why the killer left the body up there."

"Not enough room to sneak a certain valuable through, either." He rapped his knuckles across the bars.

"But why not just dump the body down here?" I said, ignoring my sidekick. "It's almost as if whoever killed Robert wanted him found."

"That's for you to figure out." Alan turned to face me. "Remember our deal. Don't get in my way and I won't get in yours.

And when we find the item, it's mine. What's that look on your face?"

"*Item.*" I burst out laughing. "You keep calling it that. I know you're looking for a fancy gold framed painting."

In only a trace of light, I caught his eyes revealing a shadow of frustration. "Titus hired you too, huh?"

"Not exactly. But he's still on my list of suspects, and he's getting impatient with your lack of progress."

"I had a feeling." Alan exhaled deeply and sucked in his abdomen, just barely squeezing past the steel. After dusting himself off, he took a step back. "Robert was quite elusive for a big guy. If he *was sneaking through here,* it must have been hell to shimmy by."

I propped against the wall, preparing to squeeze through—until something caught my eye. A small patch of fabric hung near the bottom of the opening. "Check that out. You rip something?"

Alan scanned his pants before flashing a light on the torn cloth. "Nope, not mine. I believe what we have here is a clue."

"Jinkies," I said matter-of-factly. "If this isn't from Robert... it just might be our smoking gun."

"It very well could lead to my painting. Or your killer."

"Or one and the same," I said.

I snapped a picture of the fabric and weaseled my way through the opening, mindful not to disturb the evidence. After another short walk, tiny pockets of light cut through the dark, beaming out from under a paint chipped door ahead.

Alan wrenched at the handle. "Locked." He put an ear to the door, listening intently. "This has to be it. Your turn to do some work." Lock picks waited for me in his hand.

"Finding the secret passage wasn't enough?" I took the picks and fumbled around long enough for Alan to grow restless.

The ace detective shook his head and walked over, grabbing the tools. "Let me show you how it's done."

I mumbled how I wasn't familiar with his set while he zipped through flawlessly. It was an excuse—he was way better and I needed to brush up on my skills.

After a satisfying click, the door creaked open to the maintenance tunnels I'd already toured. This time, however, I was trespassing.

Alan stopped at the doorway, peering ahead at the dimly lit expanse of dark brown brick walls and rattling pipes. "I feel like a fool for asking this now. Do they have any cameras down here?"

"Didn't your company have the Mayview contract just recently? You're in the dark in more ways than one."

"Touché—partially. Mrs. Cunningham gave us little access to the mall. Near the end, we were down to a skeleton crew of two men on the inside and two patrol cars. To be honest, it was mutually beneficial that she terminated our services. It was a pain to staff such a small account and her insistence on keeping that bumbling kid caused enough issues."

I walked past the super sleuth, deeper into the humid underbelly of the mall. "You must be talking about Bart. Good kid. And no. No cameras."

"Anything else we need to look out for?"

"Just the occasional mall ghost. Or a janitor or two."

"Great." Alan walked to a row of rusty filing cabinets, peeking behind. "According to Titus, that painting is pretty big. Five by four feet. Shiny gold frame. Can't be too easy to hide."

I crossed my arms, watching the gumshoe scurry about, checking behind every crevasse. He noticed the lack of assistance and shot a dirty look. "You gonna help here or what?"

I laughed. "As far as I'm concerned, my work here is done. I've already confirmed the killer could have used the tunnels to sneak in and out undetected. I never said I'd help look for your damn painting."

Another eye roll from the younger man. He made it look cool, too. "Fine, if you help, we'll split the take. Sixty, forty."

I pondered the offer. Any extra cash could help furnish my new office. Even more alluring was getting in with Titus. Returning the family heirloom would put me in his good graces. A connection like that would do wonders for my career—assuming he wasn't a cold-blooded killer, that is. "Fifty." I paused with a smile, seeing how desperate the man was. "And you help with my hunt for the killer."

He took a few seconds before nodding and extending his hand.

I accepted, and pulled him closer. Our handshake unbroken, I raised the stakes. "I'm getting full access to the cameras on or near the steakhouse. Everyone in and out. Everything you see, I see," I said, studying his reaction.

He smiled and nodded, ending the contract with a firm shake, full of respect. I hoped.

"I like the way you think," he said. "I would have messaged my tech guys to scrub the surrounding cameras outside, but I'm getting zero reception down here."

"You thinking someone snuck the painting out, too?"

"Not exactly. That opening was much too small. The frame was custom, solid gold. No way to cram it through. But if I can confirm someone else snuck down here, that gives me another lead. For now, I have to assume Robert stashed it somewhere here. Look for anything large and gaudy."

"Let's split up, we can cover more ground. Meet back in an hour."

We went our separate ways. I headed toward what I believed was the manager's office, while Alan took the opposite end, tracing the underground path to the security room. Luckily, our blueprint photos were stored offline, letting us use our phones as digital maps in the signless catacomb-like tunnels. Okay, they weren't that scary, but they were dark, stinky, and had countless rooms branching every which way.

I tread lightly, searching each little auxiliary room and dark corner. While an increased risk of a B&E charge was worth it to access Alan's resources, each passing minute felt like I was getting further from my main goal. Thoughts of Debbie in handcuffs flashed across my mind while I rooted through a giant laundry bin filled with old mall uniforms from the eighties. Surprisingly, they were brand new, although they took on the smell of the steamy pipes above. More fruitless searches in the stillness of the underground, the ambient hissing and clanking occasionally broken by the loud rumble of the boilers. Zooming in on the blueprint photo, I guessed I was near an exit leading to the food court.

The growing smell of tacos and General Tso's confirmed I was right, the aroma stronger with each step toward the beige exit waiting at the top. My Casio showed it was a few minutes after nine, soon after the mall's closing hours. I decided the risk of getting caught was low enough and pushed the door to peek out. As expected, I was looking at the hallway leading to the food court, the opening directly in front of the manager's office. If someone knew these tunnels well enough, they could sneak around the whole mall like the killer, or killers, in the movie *Clue*—a reminder of what Debbie said days before. And as I learned from Bart, some of the doors were so well hidden, you would only know they were there if you were looking. In fact, I wouldn't know this one existed if not for my little trip.

I shut the door and backtracked to our meeting point, satisfied there were no paintings in my path. Coming up empty worked in my favor, adding more incentive for Alan to look at the camera footage for more clues.

I wandered around for a few minutes until the overdressed man sauntered over, shaking his head. "No dice here. Except this." He held up a crumpled piece of paper. "Found under a mattress in a makeshift apartment. It's from a pawnshop dated a few weeks ago."

I caught the familiar logo on the wrinkled slip. Just my luck. It was for Corey's shop. I didn't flinch. "Robert was living down here for a bit. You think he pawned it without your guys knowing?"

"I find it incredibly unlikely... but let's find out. And get the hell outta here."

Chapter 30

"PAWN AND MORE, we're almost closed," Corey answered.

"Hey bud, I'm on my way to your shop right now." I took a slow turn out of the mall parking lot, watching Alan's truck close behind.

"Uhm, okay. Thanks for the notice. You don't have to announce your arrival, you know. I liked our sitcom style drop-ins." I heard him palm the phone to answer a customer's question. "See ya in a bit."

"Wait!" I yelled, hoping to catch him before he hung up. "I need a favor from you."

A slight pause and Corey responded. "Go ahead."

"I'm coming in with Alan Langstreet."

"Oh, this is going to be good, isn't it?" Corey laughed. "Working together?"

"I'll tell you all about it later. But for now, just follow my lead."

I gave Corey a rundown of my plan, to which he hesitantly agreed to after some convincing. After the call, and about fifteen minutes of rocking out to a few eighties new wave hits, I arrived at Pawn and More with Alan in tow. Hopefully, he made good on the promise to get his techies on the perimeter cameras—I had a lot banking on it.

Our stride through the double doors felt natural, but I was nowhere near wanting a partner long term. From Alan's relaxed posture and facial expression, I imagined he was already setting up my benefits package at Robust Robin.

"Welcome. We're closing soon guys. How can I help you?" Corey said while polishing an oil lamp that was easily older than anything in the store.

Without a greeting, my eager almost-partner flashed the pawn slip before setting it on the glass counter. "Here to collect."

My longtime friend and pawn owner grabbed the paper, holding it to the light with curiosity. "Oh, almost to the cutoff." He turned to his laptop and typed away. "With interest, that'll be... let's just make it an even five hundred."

Alan looked over with a smug grin and pulled out a leather money clip. He thumbed through the bills, taking his time to count. "Can I see it first?"

"Of course." Corey disappeared to the back then returned with a small wooden box.

Alan's face filled with disappointment. Not the giant gold framed painting he hoped for.

Corey opened the container to reveal a gleaming silver watch. "Polished it real good, too."

Alan flung the money and grabbed the container without saying a word. Mumbling something under his breath, he stomped his way out of the store. Before following the disgruntled detective, I winked at my friend as he shook his head, looking similarly upset.

As I've established, in this line of work, lying is just part of the job. It came easily, probably due to the acting background, but deep down, my ethics were always in flux. And this time, it was even easier. The insanely expensive painting in the back of Corey's shop was my only leverage for seeing the camera footage that might clear Debbie's name. And after all this blew over, I promised myself, and Corey, that I would make things right.

I jogged up to catch Alan on the way to his truck. "Bummer! Hopefully your guys find something on the cameras!"

He looked at the wooden box then back at me, eyes twitching with a hint of red.

"There's still a chance of finding it, you know. Let's see what your team can dig up. They must have found something!" I was laying on the optimism, thick.

"Yeah. They're on it." He opened the door to the extended cab and tossed the box in the backseat, then hopped into the truck. "Come to my office tomorrow. I'm sure we'll have something by then."

While my plan worked just as intended, I wondered if Alan would have helped if that pawn slip gave him what he wanted. I sat in my car for ten minutes before Crockett's theme played over the speakers. The contact wasn't saved in my phone, but I recognized it was Detective O'Connor's number.

"Little Nero's Pizza," I said with a smile.

"Can it," the policewoman said. "You got anything for me?"

I cleared my throat and looked around the parking lot, assuming I'd see her watching from a distance. "Ladies first. You called after all."

"Okay, but remember our agreement. We found her."

"Julie?" I asked.

"Yeah. Just outside Chicago."

"Deep dish isn't *that* good."

"You want intel, or an audience member?" She was irritated.

"Okay, sorry. What's she doing down there?"

"Wish I knew. A Jane Doe in one of their hospitals matched our bulletin. She's been in a coma for almost two days. Docs are saying she's lucky, if you can call it that."

I leaned back hard into my seat. "Wow. What happened?"

"Early reports look like someone tampered with her brake line. My contact down there is surprised her vehicle made it that far."

"Odd time for a road trip."

"Odd indeed. Either way, it doesn't sound like she'll be talking for a while. We're hoping she pulls through. She's our only lead."

"What if she wakes up with amnesia, like in that—"

"Stick to the real world, Paul. Oh, and I almost forgot. Coroner's report came back on Robert. Blunt force trauma, as suspected."

"Appreciate the info. Sounds about right."

"The report says the body was moved and the scene appears staged. I'm going to need more than that to get your girlfriend free, but my gut says she didn't drag her two hundred pound plus uncle out there. Well, at least by herself."

"Awesome!" I said with way too much enthusiasm.

"What's that? Tell me you got something."

"Give me the night, and I'll give you the world."

O'Connor was hesitant, eventually agreeing to wait until tomorrow after my promises of cracking the case. I was sure things were starting to line up. I thought back to Ms. Schumacher's fifth-grade classroom. "Know the five Ws." She would repeat. "And the How, too." Little did she know, those shiny plastic posters lining her walls would become a core memory of this detective. I had the When, the What, and the How. Part of the Where. I just needed the Who and the Why. All my chips were resting on that camera footage. If I could prove someone else snuck in, it's likely they clocked Robert with that fatal blow and moved the body. Channeling a bit of my own gut instinct, I had a strong feeling the old uncle's demise happened in the manager's office. Now to prove it.

Having to wait another night felt like torture, but it couldn't have been as bad as what my tangerine dream was facing. Although if tonight was anything like the last, sleep would be just as elusive. I decided to take a detour before heading home, in hopes of spending a few hours cleaning my new office. The contractors were amazing, but the pile of drywall and junk was not. They probably left the mess in spite. I gave specific instructions—I needed first crack at the *Mortal Kombat II* arcade machine. Yeah, I had more than one machine waiting, wrapped in plastic.

I turned up the jams and headed downtown, eager to see how the paint was settling. The fun solo singalong hit a snag.

Inching towards midnight, I was one of the few cars on the road—making it easy to spot the Saturn S Series tailing behind. The late nineties model sedan was in rough shape; even in the low light of the street lamps, its faded black chassis revealed a smorgasbord of dents and dings. I decided to have some fun, taking an assortment of twists and turns while still heading to the city. The dirty-windowed sedan followed, now obvious with just the two of us on the road and not much distance. Paranoia, *or was this the real deal?* In all my years of the shadow game, I'd never been on the other end of a hunt. *At least not that I knew.* Setting aside the thrill from having my first tail, I hit the gas and blew past a stop sign I knew I could safely ignore. My DeLorean was no spring chicken, but that baby could top 88, easy. And after a few quick turns and a hop on the freeway, my trivial pursuit was over.

Heart pumping to the bass of an outrun track, the open midnight road flew beneath. Long stretches of pavement melted with the music. I lost myself in the scattered headlights of opposing traffic, mixed with darkness like a scene from Lynch's *Lost Highway.* At two in the morning I glanced at the clock, realizing I'd been floating adrift for the last ninety minutes. Just like my early years, when gas was cheap and responsibilities were nil—driving around blasting tunes alone or with a friend was a favorite nighttime event. The euphoria of warm summer air almost made me forget the shadow I left behind. I convinced myself running was the safer option—a late night confrontation could've bought me a one-way ticket to the morgue. Just like in the great detective movies, I took it as a sign I was getting close. And along with the sign that read *Toledo, Ohio,* I took the first exit, sights set on my return to Motown.

Chapter 31

AFTER FINDING no strange things afoot at the Circle-K, I made my way back on the freeway, fully fueled in both car, and snack. I stuffed the empty Hostess wrapper in the console, telling myself I would get the car detailed as soon as the case was over. The summer air became chilly, helping me stay awake until the gas station coffee worked its magic. While the ride to Detroit wasn't as nostalgic, it cleared my head—like when you'd hit the degauss button on an old computer monitor, making it all warbly until it was clear again.

It was almost five in the morning when I parked near the Robust Robin office. I used my crack detective skills—along with asking the night guard—to deduce Alan wasn't in yet. With the sun only flirting to rise, I set a quick alarm before I leaned the driver's seat back and closed my eyes.

With no help from the DeLorean, I traveled forward two hours in time. I woke to the big glowing ball of gas piercing its rays through my windshield. Wiping sleep from my eyes, I set wobbly feet to concrete, gaining my sea legs and working out the cramps from the awkward snooze. Before I made it to Alan's office, my phone buzzed with an incoming call.

I wished it was a flip phone and hit a single button to accept the call. "Hi dad," I said groggily, taking a step back to lean against the building.

"Paul." Dad was stern. Not uncommon, but the early morning call was. "Your mother saw you on the news last night."

Of course. I threw my head back. After discovering a kink in my neck, I returned to the phone. "Who says there's nothing good on TV these days?"

A rare chuckle from the former cop. "She's worried about you."

"You aren't?"

He was quick with a response. "Doesn't matter what I think. I figured that out a while ago, son. Just be careful."

"You know it, dad."

"Oh, and that O'Connor's one of the good ones. I worked with her old partner. She's a firecracker. It's too late for you to join the academy, but get in good with her, and you'll see some real police work."

The call was brief. Through the hardened man's tone and trash talk, I could see he cared about me. Peeling back those layers only took a few decades. Along with me growing up—well, as much as I could. After all, I'm still a Toys R Us kid at heart.

Before putting my phone away, I replied to Corey's anxious text then wandered into Robust Robin, ready to make things right. *And hopefully,* get to the thrilling conclusion of a mystery.

I sauntered in as a welcomed guest, a nice change from the last visit. After closing the door to Alan's office, I plopped onto a comfy chair. "Tell me you've got something."

"Good morning, sleeping beauty. Got a case of the Mondays?" He tilted his head with a coy grin. "I was wondering when you'd be up."

"Car beds were all the rage growing up. What can I say?"

"On to business." He walked over and spun the sizable MacBook screen. A black and white shot of the steakhouse and surrounding shops stared back. "Watch." The ace detective hit the keyboard and leaned back as the video played. The time codes on the bottom left showed the recording played in increments of twenty seconds. Surprisingly clear for an outdoor camera, the quality was impressive.

"Where did you get this?" I asked.

"Olive Garden across the way." He pointed back to the screen. "Just watch."

The video was still for seconds, appearing frozen if not for the flashes occasionally blinking from the main road in the distance. Suddenly, a dark sportscar appeared, glitching across the screen like a video game struggling with the frame rate. It quickly found its way into a parking space on the far side of the old building. Alan leaned in, hovering a finger above the keyboard. Timed perfectly, he paused, the still shot revealing Tiffany's husband exiting the vehicle—Wyatt Price's pixelated face frozen in a permanent, cryptic scowl.

"And that, my friend," Alan started, "is all she wrote."

First came the relief, then the smile. "It's going to be really difficult for him to explain this. What happens next?"

Alan resumed the recording. Wyatt continued his glitchy path, teleporting to the back of the abandoned restaurant. A few more taps sent the video to an hour later, showing the man scurrying back to his car.

"Well, well, well. Not looking good for him," I said.

"I hope you're satisfied. After the cops pick him up, I'll get with my contact and see what Mr. Price knows about my painting. But first, I'm going to pay another visit to that pawnshop. I think that owner is hiding something. I didn't want to lose my cool back there, so I walked it off. Cooler heads prevail, my life coach says."

I let out a nervous chuckle. "Funny story, ole pal."

After stumbling over a poorly worded analogy using the plot of *You've Got Mail,* where one of the main characters deceives the other until the very end, I switched to yet another awkward analogy.

"Remember how in *Dumb and Dumber,*" I started. "The guys are running out of money, struggling on a little motorbike on the way to Aspen?"

Alan blinked, otherwise motionless and silent.

"And then they realize the briefcase they've had the whole time is loaded with money?" I let out a nervous chuckle.

"Washington! How long have you had my painting?"

I told him everything. Alan wasn't happy I lied, but after a long pause, I knew he had more respect for my detective skills.

"You know how to play the game." He tipped an imaginary fedora of his own.

Chapter 32

AND JUST LIKE THAT, the puzzle pieces tumbled together, making a beautiful Memphis pattern—like the kind on the carpet in Hopping Harvey's Hangout. I waited in the aging arcade, playing the Addams Family pinball machine close to the entrance.

"Odd place to meet," O'Connor said over my shoulder. "And you're terrible at pinball." The policewoman let out a chortle as the ball went straight down the drain.

I let go of the machine and gave her my full attention. "Figured you might want to play a round."

"Cut to the chase, and this better be good."

I pulled out my cell and played the footage Alan had graciously emailed.

"What am I looking at here?" she asked.

I walked her through the timeline of events: Wyatt arriving at the steakhouse, sneaking undetected through the tunnels, knocking Robbie out, then moving the body back through the tunnels to dump him outside.

"And then," I continued, "he messed with the building's power, wiped the cameras, and snuck around and out, all using the tunnels. Hypothetically, if someone were to go down there, they might even find a piece of fabric, torn from our killer during the escape."

She scoffed at my use of *hypothetically*. "And all this happened while you were there. Right under your nose?"

"Julie was our distraction. Remember, she stopped by right when the power went out."

The seasoned detective shook her head. "You know we can't use this footage if you stole it."

"Owner provided it to us with no strings attached." I winked.

"The local news is going to have a field day with this one."

I propped my feet on the ottoman then took a swig of Geri's latest neon colored concoction. "Lime... mint... what else am I tasting?"

"Elderflower. Some people taste green apple or pear. Filled with antioxidants, and it's said to have high anti-inflammatory properties."

"Why's it glittery?" I asked.

"Because I added glitter." Geri mixed her drink with a curly straw. "So it was your boss's husband all along? Figures, I guess. What happens next?"

I hesitated before the next swig, wondering if the shiny specs were edible before remembering everything my neighbor used was organic. "Case is pretty solid. O'Connor said they can't hold Debbie with this much doubt. She should be out soon."

"So your dream girl is safe."

I released a long sigh and stared at the jungle of plants behind the botanist. *"My dream girl is safe."*

Geri's eyes narrowed. "I'm surprised you haven't rushed out to see her."

The thought had crossed my mind, at least a dozen times. Maybe on top of a skyscraper, a slow fade-in reveal, the Tom Hanks to her Meg Ryan. Minus the kid.

I bit my lip and focused on the glass, swirling the ice cubes in a circular motion.

"I don't have to be a former psychotherapist to recognize that look. You're still thinking about Jennifer."

"Earth guys are easy too, huh?" I said.

"You need to have a proper talk with your ex-wife. I know you still care about each other. You always will. But it's okay to move on. She has. You don't need her permission, but maybe a talk can give you some closure."

I shifted in the cushion, letting her words sink in.

"And," she continued, "you might have something with the mallrat. It would be a pity to let that go. Assuming you don't find more ways to lovebomb her. I mean, c'mon, she'll appreciate being free, but your laser focus on this case was kinda..."

I tried to interrupt. "Yeah but—"

She didn't let me finish. "You ever think that your obsession with the past is holding you back from the present?"

The words were a gut punch. One that I needed to hear, even though it hurt like hell. "I'll give Jennifer a call."

I gave myself the day for some R&R. That meant plenty of futzing with my VCR to get *Lethal Weapon 2* to play. Something had put me in the mood for a good buddy cop flick. After adjusting the tracking for far too long, I collapsed into the beanbag chair, glancing at my phone.

Bart had called earlier, thanking me for clearing Debbie's name, and to say how much he enjoyed our short time together. Nice kid. I hadn't heard a peep from the newly released woman, but I wasn't expecting it. Spending a few days in a cell warranted time to process, especially considering the circumstances.

And I had one other thing on my plate today—a lunch date with my ex. Geri was more excited than I was. My neighbor was clearly tired of hearing about the past, and I'll admit, so was I. She was right, I needed closure.

Just before the end of the movie, my cell phone rang. O'Connor. Although she wouldn't outright admit it, we actually made a decent team—even if indirectly. Maybe my dreams of being a consultant to the police would be a reality. *What would my show be called?* I waved goodbye to Magnum P.I. and Shawn Spencer and returned to reality.

"To what do I owe the pleasure?" I answered.

"I wanted to follow up. Media is all over this, so the D.A. has us on overtime and working fast. It's not official, but I can safely say *case closed*. Thought you should know everything checked out."

I paused the action flick and gave myself a literal pat on the back. "Not bad for a private dick, aye?"

She ignored the question. "The knucklehead even tried to pin it on his wife. Her alibi is solid, though. They found Wyatt's prints all over the body. And his DNA on the fabric you *hypothetically* spoke of. He's going away for a long time."

I let the words marinate.

"Hey," Sara Not-Connor said. "You hearing me?"

"Yeah, so Tiffany's clean?" I wasn't surprised to hear the man accuse his wife. Something felt off from the get—the woman in the red dress, the trope that wouldn't die.

"You sound shocked. If she's hiding anything, she did a damn good job. Wyatt's claims are all circumstantial. Nothing would hold up, and like I said, alibi. The plumber confirmed she was home, but he had a hazy memory on the hubby. Oh, and Julie is out of her coma. I'll bet you can guess what she said."

I took a shot in the dark. O'Connor confirmed the Hot Topic employee received an urgent call from Wyatt to go to the mall, including instructions to keep a certain someone distracted until she got the signal.

"Inconceivable!... I mean, irrefutable," I said. "That solves it, huh."

"That solves it," she repeated. "And one more thing. Thanks."

The line went dead as my smile grew twice as large. I relaxed deeper into the bag of beans, staring at Danny Glover paused on my old CRT screen. "I'm definitely not too old for this..."

While the last few days were a rollercoaster of emotion and a drain on this forty-year-old body, it was the most fun I'd had in years. The only downside was the rough stop—the roller coaster eventually ends and the amusement park employees rush you off. I didn't know what I was expecting, but with the case snapped shut so suddenly, I was left with whiplash holding on to the exit rail. It didn't feel real. It didn't feel right. Like a writer struggling to finish their story and just forcing an ending. I won't name any TV shows, but you know who you are.

I guess I have to get used to this feeling if I'm going to take the bigger cases. Or back to the minors—cheaters and scammers.

The cell phone buzzed, almost vibrating itself off the dresser. A reminder it was nearing time for the big date. Why did I listen to Geri again?

Chapter 33

THE SMELL of her perfume found me first, even before I saw her. *Where did I smell that recently?*

"Jennifer," I said, settling in a chair across from my ex-wife. "You remembered how I like my coffee. Thanks."

"Black like the inside of a coffin on a moonless night," she said, imitating *my imitation* of the late great Chris Farley from the underrated classic, *Beverly Hills Ninja*. "You're welcome, Paul." She flashed that warm smile I fell in love with. "I'm glad you finally returned my calls. I've been worried about you."

She was wearing one of her signature form fitting sleek skirts—my original woman in the red dress.

"I've been... a bit busy." I took a swig from the cup. Yup, she knew my order—cold and extra bitter.

"Looks like it." Her tone was filled with concern. "I saw you on the news. Are you okay?"

"Yeah." My eyes darted around the coffeeshop—empty, aside from the baristas debating the most powerful anime character. "I'm sorry I've been avoiding you."

"I thought we ended things as well as we could. You know I still love you, just..."

"Not like that." I finished her sentence with a sad smile. "I know. The heart wants what the heart wants."

"Yeah. Geri tells me you have a crush."

"Geri!" I said a few notches too loudly, drawing attention from the staff. I lowered my voice. "Sorry."

"Did you forget I'm dating one of her best friends?" She looked down at her drink for a moment, her sparkly eyes soon floating back to mine with confidence returning. "You can see other people too."

I laughed. "I don't need your permission."

"Dating is weird, I know. I'd love to meet this new lady of yours."

"As long as you don't steal her away from me." My words lingered in the air before we both broke out in laughter.

"I miss you Paul. I've been meaning to thank you. Your idea for Prints of Prince was a hit. We have four cruise ships doing it weekly now. Art is selling through the roof."

"Glad to hear it. So business is good? I heard you left that big gallery and went off on your own."

A soft nod. "I have even more of an appreciation for your hustle now than when we were together. Owning a business is tough work. I joined a local group for business women a few months ago. They've been a real support, helping with my goals, and the divorce."

At that moment, I suddenly realized the roller coaster wasn't over. The end of the ride was a fake-out—the floor plummeted from underneath, sending me zipping down on the drop tower. The tadpole in my throat became a full grown *Battletoad*.

Jennifer's head cocked forward, eyes narrowed. "Are you okay? Your face..."

It was tingling, probably pale. I traced teeth over my lower lip. "That group you mentioned, it wouldn't have Tiffany Cunningham in it by any chance, would it?"

Unsurprisingly, Tiffany was avoiding my calls. So another shopping trip was in order.

Bart waved from above, leaning hard on the glass railing. "Hey boss! Didn't think I'd see you back here so soon!"

I skipped the escalators and ran up the staircase, imagining I was trying to get a piece of that radical rock on *Guts*.

Bart waited to greet me on the second level. "Did Mrs. Cunningham invite you back? Her husband was so angry the last time you were here. Now we know why!"

"I guess we do." I shrugged.

"Thanks again for all your help with Miss Debbie. It's a shame they didn't mention you on the news."

Bart knew some of what happened behind the scenes. But officially, the public eye saw O'Connor take all the credit. *Hopefully, it meant she would send more work this way.*

"All in a day's work, Bart," I said. "Tiffany here today?"

"Yes sir, probably in the manager's office. I'm on my way to the food court. Let's head on over."

Bart gave the low-down on the last twenty-four hours at Mayview. More questioning from the police, specifically Tiffany. "They grilled Mrs. Cunningham for a while. I bet they figured she was involved, but she said she got the all clear. I heard her husband has been making up all sorts of stories. The police finally left this morning. Poor Mrs. Cunningham. Losing her uncle and finding out her husband did it. At least she has her sister back."

"Poor Mrs. Cunningham, indeed," I said with a heavy layer of sarcasm before parting from the security guard.

The hallway to the manager's office was drafty—colder than I remembered. Before knocking on her door, I stole a glance at the plain beige panel across the way. The blink-and-you'd miss-it secret entrance to the maze underneath. I shook my head and waited. No answer to the knocks.

Trying the door, it was unlocked.

The chair creaked as Tiffany jumped and pulled out her earbuds. "What the hell are you doing here?"

"Good afternoon to you, too." I smiled. "I hear you've been busy."

"I thought I told you we were done." She crossed her arms, fire in her eyes. "My husband was arrested, in case you didn't hear. Killed my uncle and was stealing from the mall." Her pupils narrowed. "Some help you've been, detective. Haven't you seen enough?"

"I just can't get enough." I strolled over to the front of her desk and took a seat. "You must be pretty broken up about Wyatt, huh?"

Her hands shot out with an outstretched shrug. "Didn't I just say that? Why are you still here?"

I leaned in the chair and crossed my leg, pulling a knee in close. "White. Diamonds."

Her head snapped sharply to the side. "Excuse me?"

"You thought you were hiring a loveless private eye that was in way over his head. Easy to manipulate."

Her teeth scraped audibly as her cheeks tightened.

I relaxed even more in the chair. "Let's rewind the tape. You've got a problem. You can't sell the mall unless your sister agrees. Uncle Robbie is underwater in debt and has wanted to sell for years. He's on board. Debbie, on the other hand, she's actually doing well in that cute, cozy little bookstore."

"What are you talking about—" Tiffany squirmed, adjusting her boring grey blazer.

"Hear me out. So you have an idea. If your little sister gets caught taking a five finger discount from the mall, well, your mom drops her outta the will. That leaves you and your uncle calling the shots."

A bead of sweat trickled down my former client's cheek. "Are you done yet?"

"Oh, just you wait." I chuckled. "So you hire a dummy detective. Plant me at the scene as an eye witness to position wherever you want. Add in some video footage showing Debbie leaving the office. Boom, you have your thief. But you weren't expecting dear old Uncle Robbie to show up that night, were you?"

"I'm going to insist you leave." She fumbled out her phone, not yet dialing. "This is insane."

"It really is. So what next? The tipsy night owl catches you stealing from your own safe, doesn't he? He wasn't keen on the plan. You panic. You grab the first thing you can find… perhaps the trophy that's mysteriously missing from that case over there." I thumbed in the direction of the shelf. "You swing, knock him out. He stops breathing. You panic some more. Your sister will be coming by any minute, so you give your husband a ring. But Bart's outside, you have a bumbling detective inside, and there are cameras all over. Then you remember the tunnels, right? You've been planning to level the place, you've seen the blueprints. So hubby sneaks in through the old steakhouse. Together, you move the body through the tunnels, undetected. You need a distraction, though. So Wyatt rings his young side chick, Julie. Gives you enough time to wipe the mall's cameras. And then, you both sneak away under the mall, scot-free. Or that was the hope."

Her jaw was tighter than Lucas with the plot of *The Empire Strikes Back* in 1980. She stood, finally erupting. "The police already tried all this. This isn't one of your stupid cop movies. If you don't leave right now, I'll have you arrested for harassment."

"You're right, this is one of the *good flicks*." I sucked air through my teeth, ignoring the threat. "There's one thing I couldn't figure out. How did you know about the other exit? The abandoned steakhouse, wild, but that one made sense from the blueprints. But the cellar of the locksmith's shop. That's something you could only *dream up*."

Tiffany's face was beet red. "How did you..."

"The perfume." I smiled. "Those oh-so familiar sleek dresses from a specific local boutique. A lonely private dick. And it all started from a chance meeting at the business women's group. To quote the great Ian Fleming, once is happenstance. Twice is coincidence. But three times? Oh no, this was enemy action. Your cold call and immediate flirting was *sus*, as the kids say. But modeling yourself after my ex to have me distracted? Now that was some deep Kaiser Soze level trickery." I let out a stream of air and cracked my knuckles. "The only problem, I took a shine to your sister, not you, dollface."

And, also like the movies, O'Connor arrived seconds later, cuffs at the ready.

My gut had told me Tiffany was bad news from the start. In this game, that gut can make or break a case. And give indigestion, if you have too many coney dogs. In the end, it turns out that hiring this "bumbling detective", as she screamed on her way down the escalator, was her undoing. And just like that, my first big case was closed.

With the ride finally over, I had built up quite an appetite. I decided to have a meal at the food court, now that I wasn't banned from my childhood mall. Bart and Hakim joined, eager to try the new sandwich shop that had recently held its grand opening.

Bart opened his mouth to talk, bits of lettuce dropping onto the table. "This is so exciting. Finally, a new place to eat." He wiped his mouth after seeing our reactions. "Sorry. I'm glad Miss Debbie fought to get this sub place here."

Hakim nodded and finished a bite of his wrap. "She really does care about this mall." He looked over at me. "I'm glad she's going to be back soon. I'm minding the store while she takes the week off."

"I don't blame her." My focus drifted past the hungry men to the wall behind. Two rows of photographs stared back—glossy pictures of a dozen individuals and early mall exteriors, most in black and white. Large gold nameplates under each photo included a small description, the font too tiny to see from the table. Scanning past the first three, I paused, happy to see the kind-hearted, soulful voiced janitor mixed with the group of mall history.

"What are you smiling about, boss?" Bart asked, this time sauce dripping on his lunch tray.

"It's cool to see Forrest up there with all the mall history. How long has he been working here now?"

Both men stopped chewing, squinting in confusion. They gave each other a look, then turned to inspect the wall.

"Wait, Gus?" Bart pointed his thumb at the photo. "That's not Forrest. That's Augustus Night. He worked here for decades. Mall's first custodian. Way before my time, though. Rumor is he passed away in the arcade. This food court replaced it years later. "

All I could do was shake my head and smile.

Epilogue

POUNDING on my door interrupted an impromptu viewing of *The Shining*. I paused the screen on an empty ballroom and set down the mysterious package.

"You'll have to wait," I said to the brown paper wrapped box.

Geri opened the door before I had the chance to answer. "I get you're in your feelings, but watching *Sixteen Candles* on full blast is not the answer."

After catching my confusion, then realizing I was not watching the eighties classic, she took a step back and laughed. I froze after peeking in the hallway and heard it too. Thompson Twins echoed through the building.

Geri nuzzled my side. "She's waiting for you, idiot." The eager friend grabbed my shoulder to force me out the door. Warm afternoon air tickled my face before the sunlight. A red Focus parked by the curb, blasting the final song from the older coming of age flick. Debbie didn't say a word, leaning against the car with hands in her pockets, eyes locked on yours truly.

Frozen again in shock, my eyes widened. The brunette smiled with a soft wave in my direction. Instinctively, I looked behind to find Geri howling in delight. Focusing back to my dream girl, I pointed at myself in confusion, inaudibly asking, "*Me*?"

"Yeah, you," my crush said with a sparkling grin.

I skipped down the stairs, meeting her at the bottom of the steps.

"Hi," we both said awkwardly before taking turns with a second attempt at the greeting.

After the chuckles, I lost myself in her eyes. "What are you doing here?"

"I heard you were here."

"You came here for me?" I asked.

"Is that okay?"

"Yeah it's okay." I smirked. My eyes dodged hers. "I just didn't expect..."

She cut me off. "That both of us memorized the best ending in cinema history?"

The smile on my face was uncontrollable. "At least the 80s, for the 90s, *T2* takes the cake. Wait, do you have a cake in there? It's going to melt."

Wavy brown hair swayed as she shook her head with a goofy smile of her own. "Thanks for getting me outta jail."

"Thanks for coming over."

Her pupils darted to the side as her body relaxed. The sparkly hazel stars swirled back and tore into mine. "Make a wish?"

"It already came true."

PAUL WASHINGTON WILL RETURN.

THANKS!

As an indie author, I appreciate any and all of your support. Reviews really make a difference... so if you loved this, consider dropping a few words on Amazon or Goodreads, telling a friend, sharing on socials, and/or giving me a like here or there. ***143***

A big **Thank You** to my beta readers (Brion, Chay, Cait!), Trevor! for all the artwork and countless emails and text requests, my wife for putting up with all my zany ideas. And to you—all my readers out there—you are the best!

OTHER WORKS:

- Memoirs of a Lyrical Man
- It's Now or Never
- **Novella:** Mara's Song

For all the latest updates and freebies, check out my newsletter:

> Signup: www.steventemplar.com/news

www.ingramcontent.com/pod-product-compliance
Lightning Source LLC
Chambersburg PA
CBHW030413310726
48979CB00002B/392

* 9 7 9 8 9 8 9 1 5 3 9 5 4 *